Garbage man

max

New York Times Bestselling Author

monroe

Dedication

This isn't for the monsters who think they can own women.
It's for the real men who will kill to prove them wrong.

Garbage man

Prologue

ROOK

SHE TRIES TO SCREAM.

I see it before I hear it—the sharp inhale, the panic flaring in her eyes as her mouth opens and nothing comes out. Her breath goes ragged, and she twists her arm violently in the fucking asshole's grip.

But his hold tightens around her wrist. His mind—and those of the two suited gofers with him—is very much focused on getting Kylie into their Escalade that's parked in her driveway. I shouldn't be able to hear their thoughts, but I can. *Because of her.*

"Stop, Kylie," he says, already annoyed. "We don't have time for this."

The sound of her name on his lips is the final line crossed. I'm out of the Suburban before Kane can even pull it to a stop and stride up her driveway.

"Take your hand off her."

The man freezes. All three men do, in fact.

I've never seen these men. I don't know them personally,

but I know e-fucking-nough to know exactly who they work for and why they're here.

"Rook Slater," the one with eyes so light they look transparent says. "We heard some rumblings. Guess I shouldn't be surprised to see you here." A faint smile tugs at his mouth. He's enjoying this. *I will fucking kill him.*

"This doesn't involve you," the man holding Kylie's arm spits.

"Yeah," I say evenly. "It does. Because it involves her."

"She's coming with us."

"No. She's fucking not." It's all I say before I make my move. One second, my hand is empty, and the next, I'm behind him, dragging him back by his neck.

She is mine, motherfucker. And no one touches what's mine.

His grip on Kylie breaks, and my forearm locks around his throat.

And I don't hesitate then; I yank. Hard.

There's a sharp crack beneath my arm, and a wet, choking sound leaves his throat. His body jerks once, then goes slack. I hold him there a second longer, just to be sure.

Then I drop his lifeless body to the ground.

Kylie stumbles back, freed from his hold, and shock steals the strength from her legs.

The one with the creepy transparent eyes lunges, but Kane hits him mid-step—muscle crushing bone and the impact sharp enough to echo off the house. The man collapses in a heap, and Calloway has the third man pinned against the Escalade and is landing punch after punch to his face before the man can even register the instinct to fight back.

It's fucking vicious and violent, but it's necessary. And at lightning-quick speed, the speed only men like us can utilize, we ensure all three of these motherfuckers won't be opening their eyes again.

I turn to Kylie. Her wild and terrified gaze finds mine.

"Kylie," I say as calmly as I can. "We have to go."

She shakes her head, her body frozen. "What—"

"Now," I snap, urgency breaking through. "We have to go *now*."

She doesn't move. At this point, I know there won't be any talking her down or convincing her with words. I can tell by the stiffness in her posture and the rod in her spine and the panic-shakes of her hands.

But we have to go. We *have* to get the fuck out of here.

I'm going to have to take her. Whether she wants to go or not.

I close the distance between us, and her feet retreat instinctively toward the garage. It breaks my heart to see her this scared, but I have to do what I have to do.

I'm sorry, Ky. Really, I am.

"Rook," she pleads. "Please. Don't."

I step in, pin her arms to her sides, and lift her over my shoulder. She fights me—kicking, twisting, screaming—but I don't slow down.

"Rook, no!" she gasps. "Put me down!"

I don't.

Her heart beats faster as my brothers and I take her toward the Suburban with haste.

She screams and fights and cries, and I grind my jaw against the discomfort without slowing my stride.

In this moment, she believes she'll die at my hands if she doesn't escape.

What she doesn't know is how much she'll suffer under theirs if she does.

1

*W*HAM.

A face slams against the plexiglass before sliding down dramatically, and the brute who sent the poor soul into it skates away while chuckling to his teammates.

I tighten the laces on my skates and sigh before stretching my neck from side to side. I've been skating at the Concordia, Massachusetts, rec rink on Saturday evenings since I was five years old—nineteen dang years ago—and still, I'm never prepared for the violence the rec hockey league brings with it.

The Fighting Fangs and the Iron Knights are finishing up a game, and per usual, as I've been getting ready, I've drawn more than a few stares. It's as if they've never seen a woman before. *Wide eyes, gaping mouths, the whole nine yards.*

I stand and bounce on my toes to make sure there aren't any pinch points in my new skates, then pull my sweatshirt over my head and toss it in my bag.

As the final whistle blows, I move onto the ice as the men move off.

"Hey, Ky."

I glance over to find one of the more harmless oglers named Holland looking at me, his slightly goofy smile drenched in sweat as he slides to a stop at the glass next to me.

"Hey," I reply, my responding smile friendly.

"How's it going? Skating alone tonight?"

Normally, my best friend Alyssa would be lacing up her skates as we speak, and a little bit of the attention would be split between us.

"Looks that way." I shrug. "Alyssa has an assignment for her master's program due at midnight tonight. Chronic procrastinator, that one."

He laughs, nodding like it confirms something. "I could hang out if you want. Keep you company."

"Uh…that's nice of you…" I pause. There's something about the way he says it—too casual, too easy—and I shake my head as an overwhelming burn blooms across the back of my neck. I spin on my skates to face him and start slowly skating backward toward the center of the rink. "But no thanks. I'm good. Just going to do some drills and then head home."

"Yeah. Sure. See you next time," he offers with a salute and steps off the ice.

I watch him head toward the locker room with the other guys on his team, and unease flickers through me for no real reason. I tell myself it's nothing. I tell myself that, for the love of God, I need to get some good sleep tonight. Work's been a real kick to the gonads lately, and the hours I'm putting in on a weekly basis—pushing seventy—are really starting to get to me.

I do a slow spin to test the texture of the ice—only to screech to a stop when I nearly collide with something solid enough to feel like a wall.

Grumpy. Serious. Glaring.

The Garbage Man. *My* garbage man. The one I chase down the street every Tuesday morning with my bin while he waits beside his big truck, arms crossed, looking like my existence personally offends him.

Rook Slater.

"Oh. Sorry," I blurt out, trying to keep the peace even though he's the one who skated right up on me.

I know he plays hockey—everyone knows the Slater brothers are real hard-asses on the ice, and I see him here all the time—but something about seeing him this up close and personal makes my stomach drop. He normally keeps his distance.

His alluring smell at this proximity is an unexpected addiction. Even sweaty, he smells sweet, like a perfectly salted chocolate chunk cookie—completely and utterly un-garbage-man-like. I resist the urge to suck in a breath of air and swallow by focusing on his looks instead.

He's deadly handsome, I'll give him that—dark hair, dark, mysterious eyes, and a jawline born of the gods—but he never fails to look like he's swallowed a bundle of knives. Especially when he's looking at me, a task in which he's engaged fully right now.

First, my face, until his gaze tracks down my throat, my chest, and my hands before it snaps back up so fast it feels like I caught him doing something he wasn't supposed to.

He melts into both anger *and* something sharper, and goose bumps scatter up my arms and neck.

His jaw clenches. His shoulders tense. For half a second, it looks like he might say something, but just before the pinnacle of tension is released, he exhales through his nose, turns abruptly, and skates away hard and quick, like he's trying to get away from me as fast as he can.

Okay. *Rude.*

I mean, I don't know what I ever did to this guy, but clearly, he's not my biggest fan.

Whatever. My worth doesn't hinge on the guy who collects my garbage, for Pete's sake. Not that there's anything wrong with blue-collar work—actually, it's hot knowing a man is good with his hands. But Rook Slater is such a fringe part of my life, he doesn't deserve main character headspace.

I shake it off and skate toward center ice, but my focus slips as I watch Rook reach the benches and nearly tear off his skates while his brothers move toward him. Their tone is much more jovial—one of them, Kane maybe, even tosses me a wink—as their blond and brown heads respectively glint in the fluorescent light from overhead. But when they reach him, and exchange low words I can't hear, their faces turn serious.

It feels a lot like they're all watching me now, but I try really hard not to notice and just skate.

I hardly know anything about the Slater brothers despite years of running in the same Concordia circles, and they definitely don't know much about me. They can work their blue-collar jobs and play hockey on the weekends, and I'll do my own thing too because *who cares* what they're saying or thinking.

Right? Right.

I think they're a few years older than me, but to be honest, I don't really know. They all seem the same age or close, but they don't look alike at all, so it doesn't make sense for them to be triplets. It's weird. I suppose I could ask, but it never feels like the appropriate time to insert myself into potential family drama, especially given the dirty looks I already get from Rook. I have a hard time pinpointing anything that should cause so much disdain, but it doesn't matter.

It. Doesn't. Matter. Kylie.

Shaking my head to clear it, I skate a loop around the rink, foot over foot over foot until I've picked up enough speed to feel the ice-cooled air brush against my face. I do a few spins to get my footing before throwing a toe loop to get started.

I feel good, limber even, and my roommate Alyssa will be happy to hear that the stretches she's been telling me to do are paying off.

Skating is one of my favorite things in the world. Growing up, it was my escape from the turmoil that comes with losing both of your parents at a young age. Now, it's an escape from the stress and mundanity of everyday life. It's my sanity in a largely insane world, and it feels good to lose myself in the power of it rather than the uneasy feelings I get from the Slater brothers.

My phone buzzes in the side pocket of my leggings, so I slide to a stop and pull it out to get a look, just in case it's important.

Unknown: Kylie, it's Gammy. This is my new number. I lost my phone again.

I snort. My grandma is almost eighty, and has not, no matter how many times I've explained, grasped the fact that losing your phone doesn't mean you have to get a new number. You just get a new phone. I don't bother getting into that for the five millionth time now. The number will be new again within the month, and we'll have to do the whole dog and pony show all over again.

Me: Okay, I'll add this to my contacts.

Gammy: Good. Also, do you have some time to get together this week? It's really important that we talk.

This week? She's kidding, right?

I work for an accountancy firm just outside Boston, and with returns due painfully soon, this week is pure murder, schedule-wise. I love my Gammy—she's the one who raised me after my parents passed—but I don't think fitting her in at this stage of tax season is even humanly possible. I barely make time for skating, and that's practically therapy.

Me: Ah, I don't know. This week is so, so busy, Gammy. Can it wait until after the 15th?

The 15th, as in *April 15th*. Otherwise known as D Day in the tax world and a measly two and a half weeks from today.

Gammy: No. It can't.

I guffaw, but when I look up from my phone, every hair on my body stands on end.

All three of the Slater brothers are staring right at me.

Kane and Calloway have the good grace to look contrite for being so unabashed about it. Rook, on the other hand, looks like he's trying to set me on fire. The intensity of his glare makes my breath hitch and hold. As much as I want to, I can't look away.

But much longer of this staring contest, and I fear he'll be able to hear the thoughts rolling around inside my head.

What's his freaking deal? What did I ever do to him? How can a man look so angry and scary and be so hot at the same time? And for the love of everything, why can't my vagina distinguish between the two?

Eventually, I *have* to look away first. The intensity is too much.

Taking a deep breath and pouring everything I have into regaining my focus, I move my attention back to my phone and type out a text.

> **Me: Geez. Well. Okay. I'll try to figure something out and let you know, okay?**
>
> **Gammy: Don't try, Ky. DO. We need to talk.**

Geez. I want to put stock in her words, but the last time she sounded this serious, all she wanted was to warn me against the dangers of Botox. It was valid advice, coming from a woman with glass skin and an ass that won't quit even at her age, but it was hardly groundbreaking information.

I'm not saying I won't try to find a time to have dinner with her or something soon, but I definitely can't nail anything down before reading the room with my boss, Martin. He's pretty chill nine out of twelve months of the year, but as of two Fridays ago, he's smack-dab in the middle of an existential crisis.

Pretty sure it's not going to be as simple as me saying "my gammy needs me" while my boss is balls deep in IRS returns. There's going to have to be sugarcoating and coddling and working through returns at the speed of light to be able to leave the office with enough time to make the forty-five-minute drive to my grandma's house, have dinner, and be back again before midnight at any point over the next two and a half weeks.

I tuck my phone into my leggings and push off again, forcing my focus back onto the ice. I glide into motion, ready to get back to work on my toe jumps. For some reason, they're always my sloppiest, and I find starting with them when my energy is highest is the most productive.

I turn and burn around the outside of the rink, spinning around and skating backward for half the loop before spinning forward again.

But still, I'm not alone.

Across the rink, Holland and a few of the Fighting Fangs lean against the plexiglass, out of their gear and watching me without remorse. A quick glance confirms that the trio of Slater brothers has made its way to the locker room, and shockingly, in their absence, my tension over being watched only amplifies.

I try to concentrate on my form instead of on the ogling men, but the vulnerability won't leave. I'm in a sports bra and leggings, and the weight of all these eyes makes me feel like I'm in a fishbowl.

Like I'm being measured and judged and calculated somehow. I don't understand it, but it doesn't feel good.

It's probably ridiculous. *I'm* probably being ridiculous. I mean, this is a public rink in a sleepy town, and these are a bunch of hockey dudes locking in on the only woman they can.

But…the unease won't leave.

Ugh.

Why are these men so damn starved for female viewing? Don't they know there's free porn on the internet?

2

ROOK

"YOU'RE REAL SUBTLE TONIGHT, ROOK," MY YOUNGER brother Kane says. "Real calm, too."

"Oh yeah," Calloway, the baby brother of our macho brood, chimes in. "Very zen. Nothing says inner peace like skating like you want to murder the ice every time she's in the building. Though, I do wonder if there's a slightly better approach you could utilize. Maybe a little…wooing, perhaps?"

I groan. "Shut the hell up."

Kane laughs his ass off, thrilled to have gotten a reaction, and I yank the guards over my blades, shoving them into my bag harder than necessary.

"It's not like that," I continue. "And you know it."

"Oh, we know," Calloway says, peeling off his pads. He's always the calmest one out of the three of us. Where Kane is the jokester and I'm what they'd probably call *the asshole*, Cal is the closest to Buddha a vampire will ever get. "You watch her like a fucking hawk whenever she's near, bro. Kind of makes your…*circumstances*…hard to ignore."

I'm the oldest of the Slater brothers, but the way these

bastards are calling me out, you'd think the sibling hierarchy doesn't exist. Still, I find myself giving in to their nosiness.

"It doesn't fucking matter anyway. She loathes me," I snap. "Every time I open my mouth, she looks like she's bracing for impact."

"That's because you look like you're preparing to commit a felony," Kane says. "You ever try a smile? A wink, perhaps? Anything other than a sneer would do."

I zip my bag and stand. My muscles are tight as shit from all the adrenaline of the game and the awkward as fuck interaction with the female topic of the hour, and it's making my blood feel a thousand degrees hotter than it should even be capable of feeling.

Unfortunately, Kane isn't wrong. I look miserable because I *am* miserable.

One day, I was fine—I was a regular guy with a regular job and a regular set of annoying-as-fuck brothers with a special, but rarely inconvenient, biological makeup—and the next, I was a prisoner in my own body.

The second Kylie Moon stepped onto the ice a week ago—the day after I turned twenty-eight—a visceral, bone-deep reaction that locked all my senses in on her snapped into place and hasn't left since. As if her presence has the power to control me. I thought the lore I'd read about us and our ancestry and the way our love works was bullshit—that if I hated the idea of it, it wouldn't apply to me.

Turns out, it's not bullshit, and no matter how much I've tried to convince myself that I'd be different or exempt, I'm not.

I've been fighting the magnetic pull to claim her ever since. Including tonight. *Especially* tonight.

It doesn't matter that I didn't want this—that I *don't* fucking want this. I've spent my entire life bucking the rules and the expectations of the machine that chews human women up and spits them out after giving them bullshit promises of luxury and status in exchange for their sustenance. I've spent my *entire life* preparing to give it all the middle finger.

But now that I'm in the nitty-gritty of it, my body's nearly inconsolable. It's pathetic at best.

I spare myself no pity, slinging my bag over my shoulder with shaking hands, barking an order at my brothers. "Just fucking drop it."

Kane smirks at me like he can see inside my head. The fucker can't, no matter how hard he tries. That's a gift reserved for only me, it seems.

"I know you're fucking *feeling* it," he pushes, not dropping it at all. "You have to be, bro. You look at her like the whole world will collapse if you blink."

Calloway's gaze sharpens as he searches my face for answers I never wanted to have. "Just tell me this…did you feel it immediately after turning twenty-eight? Just turned on like a light switch? Or was it, like, a slow build for the last few months or something?"

I don't answer. I don't have to. The look on my stupid fucking face says enough.

Kylie Moon has always drawn attention. I saw it, even if I didn't care. But now, it's killing me to let her out of my sight, as if my body registers her absence before my mind can even justify it.

It's night and fucking day.

She's always been beautiful, but now, she's *everything*.

Kane's mouth stays shut for once, and Calloway exhales

slowly, finishing with a whistle that echoes throughout the locker room. "Okay, then. Immediate."

"Finish packing your shit and meet me outside," I snap through gritted teeth, grabbing my bag and storming out the locker room door to answer the loudening call to be near her.

Neither brother says a word as I exit because they know this isn't something we talk about lightly. Both of my brothers are Chatty Fucking Cathys every goddamn day of the week, but there's some shit you don't say out loud, *vampire* and *mate* included.

I lean against the glass, across the rink from the other *spectators*—to put it nicely—watching Kylie on the ice. She's smooth and confident, and every muscle movement is tight and controlled, like she knows exactly where her body is at all times. My body mirrors the feeling, reveling in the comfort of watching her.

She has no idea that she's being circled as prey, and even more fucked up, my desperate, choking yearn is only a small piece of it.

Holland Thorne, the Fighting Fangs's biggest piece of shit, leans against the glass on the far side, pretending to joke with the other guys on his team. He watches her closely, tracking her movements, and logging something behind his slimy fucking smile I wish I could figure out. Unfortunately, the elites have gifted him with the ability to shield, so I'm shit out of luck, despite my *heightened abilities*.

My jaw tightens. *Fuck that guy. Fuck everything about him.*

Kane, having joined me from the locker room, follows my line of sight. "He looks pretty focused over there."

Calloway nods. "He's also been asking questions."

That gets my full attention. Cal has always had hearing like a hawk. "About her?"

"Yeah. Her job. Her routines. Where she lives. Where her roommate was tonight. If she's dating anyone." Calloway's voice drops. "Any chance he can get, I hear him asking her shit. Hear him asking other people about her shit. It's nothing overt. But it feels a lot like the pattern behavior we've seen before."

Fuck. My blood spikes sharp and violent.

I know what kind of man Holland is. I know who he works for. I know where his priorities lie. When it comes to women, I know what Holland's motives are, and I really wish I didn't give a single fucking shit. But I do.

The universe has seen fit that I would.

Every abominable cell inside my goddamn body feels like it's programmed to care. I try to force the rage down, but swallowing past it feels like barbwire.

Before I know it, I find myself saying, "Keep ears on him."

Cal waggles his brows. Kane smiles like a fuckwad. The only thing they love more than giving me shit is listening to me admit I might actually need them.

"Quiet fucking ears."

"Wasn't planning on making a scene, bro," Cal says, and Kane is still grinning. "But I'll keep my ears open."

Scenes draw attention, and attention from men like Holland gets certain women killed. And sadly, because of how attuned I am to Kylie Moon, I know she's a certain kind of woman—one that attracts the men Holland works for like bees to honey.

I risk another glance at Kylie, and the bond—the *thing* I refuse to name—thrums under my skin like a live wire. Every instinct in me screams to get closer, to put myself between her and the rest of the world, to drag her somewhere safe from assholes like Holland and never let go.

I clench my fists.

You know this is exactly how it starts. You've already seen it time and time again.

Calloway watches me carefully. "You know fighting it doesn't make it go away."

"No," I say. "But it buys time."

"And what exactly will time give you?" Kane asks. I don't answer because I don't know what time buys me.

Time to figure out what the endgame is?

Time to decide how deep this goes?

Time to make sure she doesn't end up on a list she never agreed to be on?

I don't fucking know. But that's pretty on par for me these days, because I don't know anything anymore. *Besides the fact that I want Kylie Moon—and badly.*

"I'll let you know when I figure it out," I tell them instead.

"Okay, bro. Let's just keep buying time, for the sake of, you know, time," Kane teases.

"Hell yeah. Let's get more…*time.*" Cal laughs and offers me a high five. I don't accept, but he finishes the gesture himself, slapping one hand against the other.

I groan. "How about you two fuck right off."

Both of my brothers have the nerve to laugh, but I ignore them.

Across the rink, Kylie finishes a lap and slows her pace as she pushes her warm brown hair off her face. For a split second, her eyes flick toward the benches.

They land on me.

Something I don't know how to describe passes between us. It's recognition without understanding, curiosity edged with unease. *The uncontrollable pull, it seems, isn't exclusive to me.*

Taking pity on what must feel impossibly confusing for her, I look away first.

Kane claps me on the shoulder. "We're heading to the Suburban. You coming?"

"In a minute."

They don't argue. They know better when I'm in a mood like this.

When they're gone, I pull out my phone and open the note I've been adding to all week. It's not dreams or visions like I've experienced before. It's not as formal as that, but rather, fragments of something my instincts won't let go of.

Unattached Female

Stalked

Flat Tire

Private Event

Opulent Penthouse

I add one more line.

Intervene if it's Kylie Moon.

Frustrated, I drop my phone inside my bag and take one last look at her. Then I zip my bag, sling it over my shoulder, and head for the exit.

Whether I want this bond or not, whether I fight it or not, one thing is certain: I don't want *anyone* touching Kylie Moon.

Not even me.

3

KYLIE

I DON'T KNOW IF YOU KNOW THIS, BUT MONDAYS during tax season have a smell. It's a combination of burned coffee, panic-induced pit sweat, and printer ink.

By ten a.m., my boss, Martin Feldman, has already made fifteen laps around the office, his bald head shining beneath the fluorescent lights while he wears a rut in the blue Berber carpet, bitching to everyone within earshot and freaking out in nerd speak. His tie is loosened, his sleeves are rolled up, and because of the wear and tear on his loafers, he's shrunk half an inch.

"If one more client emails me asking what a 1099 is," he announces, stopping by my desk, "I'm going to fake my own death."

I don't look up from my screen. "Pseudocide would complicate payroll, Martin, and at this stage of the game, I don't need any more complications."

"Good point." He peers at my monitor. "How are you doing over here, Moon?"

"Thriving," I say. "Ever since I was a little girl, I've dreamed of having the kind of stress that causes hair loss, brittle nails, and wrinkles as a part of my career."

"Stress causes hair loss?"

I suck my lips into my mouth and point my eyes directly at his barren head. "Nooo."

He snorts. "Well, good news, if we survive the fifteenth, drinks are on me."

"And if we don't survive?" I ask, pessimistically amused.

"Burn this place to the ground with me inside it. Oh, and make sure you tell my wife I loved her." He pats my shoulder and keeps moving, already muttering about needing to file extensions for the Bergwitz, Holsten, and Smith families, and leaving no opening for me to explain that if we don't survive, my corpse won't be able to burn anything down. Or, I suppose, tell anyone that he loves them. I don't have anyone to tell besides Gammy, but boy oh boy, is that a can of worms for another time.

I have too much shit to do. Working here in the spring is the kind of busy where all you can do is brace yourself for the wild ride to hell and hope you have enough flame-retardant clothes to come out the other side. You can quite literally work at a break-neck speed and still feel behind.

After I manage to submit the twenty federal filings Martin has signed off on so far today, I step out of the office to grab a sand-wich from my favorite deli a few blocks away.

The streets are slushed from a mid-March snow and ruth-lessly cold weather, so I head for my car down the block instead of making the walk—since there's no way I can finish the workday with wet feet. A dark SUV creeps along the curb behind me, likely looking for a spot to park with all the snowbanks, and I glance over my shoulder every so often to see if they succeed. They're still idling when I return to the office—chicken salad sandwich in tow—before finally speeding off through the light and around the corner as I enter the small parking lot reserved for employees of Feldman CPA.

There are several empty spots on the street—I see that now—and a weird tingling sense of unease washes over me.

Boston traffic is a nightmare, I tell myself, brushing it off. *And it's probably not even the same SUV. Pretty sure everyone and their mother drive blacked-out Escalades around here.*

I stay busy at the office until a little after seven, when Martin decides it's time for us to go home, eat dinner, cry in the shower, and get some sleep—his real instructions at quitting time every day, by the way.

It's another forty minutes before I get home because living in Boston city center is way out of my price range. And I'm barely through the door—haven't even laid eyes on Alyssa—when my phone starts ringing. I half expect it to be Martin with a new take on postmortem care, but it's my grandmother's name on the screen.

"Hey, Gammy," I greet nonchalantly—as though I haven't been avoiding her or her request to get together for the last two days with Olympic-level agility. "How's it going?"

Guilt niggles slightly as she pauses. Normally, she's ready to dive into some kind of gossip right out of the gate, and if she's not, I can only imagine it's because she's feeling annoyed with me.

"Gam, I'm sorry—"

"Are you okay?" she cuts me off.

My chin jerks to my chest in surprise. "Uh…yeah…I mean."

I shrug to myself. "It's tax season, so I'm not *okay*, but I'm okay at the same time, you know?" I snort. "I'm surviving."

Another pause. "I know work's busy this time of year, Kyky. I mean everything else. You're sleeping okay? Eating enough? Feeling…*safe?*"

I frown as I toe off my heels, the SUV from earlier today ushering unbidden anxiety into my mind. "*Safe?* Gammy…you're starting to make me feel like things aren't supposed to be okay. What's going on?"

"I can't do this over the phone," she says gently. "I just need to see you."

I glance at the clock. "You live forty-five minutes away. I've been working twelve-hour days six days a week."

"I know," she says. "But I never get to see you, and this is important. Don't you miss me?"

I roll my eyes. *Grandmothers really have a special gift for charging every single encounter with guilt.*

"*Gammy.*" I close my eyes, feeling torn in twenty directions with no stretchy flesh to give. "That's not fair. You know I miss you."

"Life isn't fair, baby," she counters. "It's fast and furious and complicated in a thousand different ways. Come tomorrow, after work, doesn't matter how late. I'll make pot roast—your favorite *and* it can sit for hours."

I sigh. "You play dirty."

"See you tomorrow night, sweetheart," she says cheerfully, hanging up before I can argue.

I stand there for a moment, phone in hand, considering the implications of my grandmother's pushing. Either something serious is going on or I need to set parental controls on her TV. *Fast and furious? Am I safe?* I need to block Vin Diesel and true crime, like, yesterday.

Still, I don't think I can make it there tomorrow night without chancing a full-on mental breakdown, no matter how badly she wants me to.

Ugh. Whatever.

Tonight, I'm choosing peace. Tomorrow morning, I'll break the news of my continued absence and then set my phone to silent.

A disturbing visual of my roommate Alyssa, sprawled out with one leg on the back of the couch and the other draped off the edge with both hands in a bowl of cheeseballs, is the first thing I see upon exiting the kitchen.

Her laptop is closed on the coffee table, her shirt covered in orange dust, and her red hair is in a messy bun that signals the end of her latest academic ordeal. She's not a simple, happy girl when she's under the gun—but rather a stressed-out, soul-siphoning metaphorical demon—and the fall into relief afterward often looks apocalyptic.

"What's your status? Can I assume by the junk-food-indulging-bowl-of-balls that you're finished?"

"Freedom, baby," she declares, stretching and sitting up to set the bowl on top of her computer. "My paper is submitted, I am officially brain-dead, and thankfully, I don't need to worry about the next butt-puckering assignment for another three to five business days."

At which time, she will, once again, deadline-crunch at the last minute. Some cycles really are predictable.

"That's great! Want to come to the rink with me to celebrate?

I'm brain-dead too, and I need to skate off some of this anxiety or I'm afraid I'll wake up melted tomorrow."

"Hell no." She groans. "I plan to sit here and rot."

"I'll buy you dinner after. Whatever you want. Even if it's that horrible taco joint you love so much."

"Sorry, no sale." She points to a grocery bag filled with more junk food at her feet. "I plan to rot *with snacks*."

"Oh, come on, Alyssa!" I call over my shoulder as I head into my bedroom to change out of my work clothes. "It'd be nice to have a little female companionship there tonight. The hockey guys were particularly feral on Saturday."

"They always are!" she yells back to me. "They see one woman on ice and forget how to act."

I toss on a sports bra, leggings, and a hoodie before slipping on my favorite pair of runners. When I walk back into the living room, Alyssa still hasn't budged an inch, other than to move from cheeseballs to Pringles.

"You don't feel…*weird* when you're at the rink around those guys?" I question. "I mean, they stare. A lot."

"No." She shakes her head, but then a beat later, she smiles. "I mostly feel horny. Maybe a little jealous. Rook Slater always looks at you like he wants to chain you to his bedpost and have his wicked way with you, and I'd like to have my wicked way with him. Or his brothers. Any of the Iron Knights will do, really."

A laugh bursts from my lungs. "He looks at me like he wants to kill me, Al."

"With orgasms, maybe." She snorts. "A death I'd happily accept if I were in your position. It's been a long ass time since I've gotten my kitty licked."

I pick up a pillow and throw it at her. "You're foul."

Alyssa laughs her ass off. "More like, *I'm sexually repressed because school is turning me into a hermit.* I'm definitely going to need to go out this weekend and get some play. Even stray kitties need love."

I roll my eyes and laugh. "That's exactly what you said two weekends ago after you met a deadline. And the deadline before that. And the deadline before *that*."

She shrugs and pops another chip into her mouth. "Patterned desires are indicative of an underlying need, Ky. It's scientific."

Alyssa *loves* hooking up. I, on the other hand, take a more chaste—some might even say *picky*—approach to sex. Sure, I've messed around with guys, but at twenty-four years old, I've yet to find the right guy to have actual sex with. Alyssa thinks I'm batshit crazy for holding out this long, but I've never second-guessed it. For some reason, I've always felt really confident that I'll know when the time is right.

"You really don't get skeeved out by them?" I ask again, the thought looping back as a shiver runs down my spine.

"They're harmless, Ky." She waves a hand. "Just a bunch of macho cavemen."

I shrug. I guess she's right. It's not as if any of them has ever crossed a line before, and it's a little unfair of me to project my assumptions onto them without proof.

I grab my duffel from the hallway closet. "Okay, I'm out. I'll see you later."

"Have fun!" she calls toward my retreating back. "I'll just be here, rotting into the couch!"

I snort and head out the door, making the short drive to the rink with my head in the clouds. My mind races with client folders from work and ways to let Gammy down gently and hockey guys and their wandering eyes.

It's not long before I'm pulling into the parking lot of the rink and cutting the engine, and a horrible sense of not even knowing how I got here snaps me back into focus.

I've got to shed some of this stress, or I'm going to be a hunchback by the time I'm thirty.

The sky is pitch black, and the winter air hovers as I lock my car and walk inside, scanning the parking lot as a precaution. When the rink door shuts and locks behind me, restricting access to people with a membership fob of their own, I relax a little.

The rink smells like ice and rubber and sweat in a familiar and grounding way that settles a calm into my bones and reminds me why I dragged my tired ass here in the first place.

I lace up my skates and take off my hoodie, reveling in the relief that hits me as soon as my skates hit the ice.

The rink is blissfully empty, and my heart instantaneously full. There are no hockey guys finishing up a game, no shouts or bodies being violently slammed into the glass, and no expectations or deadlines to be met. There's just the low hum of the lights overhead and the clean bite of cold air against my lungs as I free myself through the movement from one end of the rink to the other.

This is exactly what I needed.

I start my laps, letting muscle memory and rhythm take over. The tension of work and Gammy and weird feelings—along with a million other weights I didn't even know I was holding—begins to loosen, and I can feel my shoulders drop as my breath evens out.

This is why I come here. This is peace. This is home.

Maybe it's because it makes me feel close to my mom and dad—they met here at this very rink and fell in love nearly thirty years ago, before they had me. Before they passed away. Maybe it's because it's the only thing I do just for me. And who knows, maybe it's even simpler—a true testimonial for the endorphins in exercise.

But whatever the reason, I'm grateful such a place exists.

I'm halfway through my fifth lap when all those good feelings start to meld with something of a different kind. It's a subtle shift—a slight raise of my now-relaxed shoulders and a tingle at the back of my neck. But it's enough to get my attention.

I slow my speed and move my eyes away from the ice and toward the plexi. I spot Holland on the other side of the glass, one shoulder resting on it casually. As our eyes meet, a soft smile spreads across his mouth.

"Long day?" he calls out toward me, and my stomach tightens a little.

How long has he been here? Why is he here? He's not dressed in hockey gear, and the Fighting Fangs don't usually practice on Monday nights anyway.

They're harmless. Alyssa's words ring out in my head, urging me to settle. Holland Thorne and I have been interacting for going on two years at this point at an acquaintance level, and he's probably trying to cross the threshold into friendly. It's not like I have to marry the guy, but it wouldn't kill me to dial down the brain drama a click or two.

"Yeah," I reply, skating toward him but stopping a few feet short, the wall still between us. "Pretty sure this is the eighty-fourth hour and counting."

He's still smiling as he pushes off the glass. "I had a feeling I'd find you here."

"You came here looking for *me*?"

He shakes his head, rounding the wall to the opening and leaning into the side of it. "Well, technically, I just finished up a workout on the ice about forty minutes ago. Practice." He shrugs and grins.

I guess they changed up their practice schedule.

"But I thought maybe you'd show up here to work out, so I hung around. I wanted to let you know about this private event thing I'm going to later this week."

"Private event?" I question, taking in the way he's dressed with sharp eyes. Suit. Tie. Perfectly groomed hair. *He must've showered after his practice.*

"Yeah. The firm I work at is having a private event on Friday night. Drinks. Dancing. Food. It's more of a networking thing, but there will be a lot of people there who like to invest in…talent. I thought maybe you'd be interested, so I wanted to invite you."

I don't know what kind of firm Holland works at, but my brows knit over the casual way he's inviting me on…a date? I don't know if that's what he's getting at, but for the life of me, I can't think of any other reason he'd be inviting me to some kind of work event for talent scouting.

"Talent?" I repeat. "What exactly does that have to do with me?"

I'm no Hollywood actress or model or singer. I'm a junior accountant who skates as a hobby.

"You skate beautifully, Kylie," he says, like it's a fact, not a compliment. "There are a lot of avenues where you could turn that talent into something else. Lots of people who'd love to uti-lize you. You've never thought about breaking away from the ac-counting gig?"

My responding laugh is quick and edged with strain. "Oh yeah. Only every tax season or so, when taking a bath with my toaster starts to sound reasonable. But not, like, seriously. For the most part, I like what I do."

His smile is easy and patient. "No pressure. Totally your call. Just figured it might be something worthy of your time. And, well, I'd be there. So, yeah." He winks. "It'd be fun too. We could hang out."

Okay, yep. There's the date part I was wondering about.

Which I'm absolutely not interested in. Holland seems nice, but he's not even remotely my type.

Though, I've never thought about finding a way to turn my love and passion for ice skating into some kind of career. And turning down the opportunity to explore that just because I don't want to lead him on feels a little hasty…

"That's really…nice of you," I answer, my voice hesitant with each word as I attempt to toe the thin line precariously placed between the two parts of me. "Can…I…uh…think about it?"

"Of course," he replies, stepping aside without protest and offering another little wink in my direction. "If you want to go, you know where to find me."

I push off again, starting up another lap to get back into a rhythm, but I only make it halfway around before meeting an-other observer.

Jiminy Cricket. So much for the rink being empty.

I slide to an agitated stop in front of Rook, who's leaning

against the bleachers. He, too, isn't wearing skates or gear, but jeans and boots instead, and his eyes bore into the back of the retreating man in the suit at the other end of the arena like he can turn him to dust with his mind.

It's oddly protective in a way I don't understand and makes the hair on my forearms stand straight up.

I *almost* go back to skating, but something inside me just says, *fuck it.*

"Can I help you?" I ask, finding my voice and doing it with challenge.

Instantly, Rook's eyes jump to mine, but that's where the concessions on his aggressive posture stop. He swallows hard before shoving off the bleachers, charging down the back wall, and leaving the rink, out the door and into the parking lot through the same door Holland took without a word.

I'm left standing there with my mouth agape and my senses tingling like a fucking idiot.

What is with *this guy?*

Suddenly, the peace and respite I felt from the ice fifteen minutes ago is gone, and the desperate need for a shower cry and the comfort of my bed has taken its place.

Cutting my drills short, I skate off the ice with angry strides and shaking hands, pulling my sweatshirt on and yanking my blades off with little to no finesse.

Alyssa would probably laugh if she were here—probably tell me I'm the weird one, not the hockey guys, and that I'm letting them get to me too much. Hell, she'd probably encourage me to go to the private event thing with Holland on Friday *and* book angry sex with Rook on Saturday, but none of that is even remotely me.

It's a little after nine when I'm stepping out of the rink, my bag slung over my shoulder and a crease in my forehead from overanalysis, and the parking lot is expectedly quiet at this time of night.

I walk toward my Civic that's parked toward the back of the lot, but pull to an abrupt stop when something throws a wrench in the plan.

Oh, come on. *You have* got *to be kidding me.*

4

ROOK

I FUCKING HATE THIS SHIT.

I hate that whatever this thing is can drag me across town without asking. Hate that I let it. Hate that I can't fight harder against it.

By the time I pulled into the rink's lot, I already knew she was here. That is, after all, what brought me here after I left Kane's place—my body choosing the direction with a swift turn of my steering wheel before my brain could weigh in.

And now, I'm still here, skulking in the dark like some kind of stalker.

Kylie Moon is halfway across the asphalt of the dark parking lot, keys in hand, bag slung over her shoulder, posture loose in the way of someone who still believes the night is normal. She doesn't notice the sound at first, but that's what makes her human. She's built for softness, for love, for life; I'm built for awareness, for speed, for execution.

We are opposites, and yet, at an intrinsic level, we are one.

A slow bleed leaks air from her tire, and a soft hiss fills the otherwise frigid night air, audible exclusively to my sensitive ears.

I'm no match for Cal, who can probably hear this shit from his couch, but my hearing, in comparison to Kylie's, is undeniably advanced.

And so is my vision. Even from here, I can see the puncture in her tire isn't from a rock or road debris. *As suspected, this was intentional, and that means someone meant it as a trap.* Anger chokes me as my vision tunnels to Kylie and her immediate surroundings.

Her brown hair is pulled into one of those messy knots she always has when she skates, a few loose strands catching the light from the moon as she walks, and her bright, entrancing blue eyes scan the lot as she holds her keys tightly in her hand. She's on edge, I can feel it in my bones, and a surge of pride for her survival instinct overwhelms me.

Humans aren't born into a perfect world any more than we are—but the societal expectations are different. *Trust easy, be kind, give the benefit of the doubt*—they live within a golden rule to treat others the way they'd like to be treated.

Vampire code is harsher but, in a lot of ways, a hell of a lot less complex. *Trust is earned. Kindness is reserved. There are no benefits—only doubts.*

We care for those who care for us, and beyond that, everyone else is a threat. Connection is weakness, and for me, Kylie Moon is my biggest fucking liability.

She isn't polished or curated, but her beauty is there in every innocent facet of her being and taking up space like there isn't a seedy world thinking it can decide who she belongs to.

I didn't come here with the intention of intervening.

I came here because I'm clearly fucking powerless against this thing I didn't choose.

Something instinctual tightens low and harsh in my chest. The need to protect it—to protect her—runs all the way to my roots. My muscles coil, focus narrowing, everything in me snapping toward her like a compass needle when *his* presence overwhelms me.

Fuck. I grit my teeth.

Not expecting Holland to be here was naïve—and since being naïve is the last thing a man like me can stand to be, I *will not* be it twice.

The slimefuck stands ten feet back from her car, leaning against a sedan that doesn't belong to him, materialized out of nowhere from the thick, foggy air he's pretending to breathe.

He looks down at the screen of his phone like he's busy with something casual rather than lurking, but I know the whole scene is too goddamn scripted to be coincidence, and that the only reason I couldn't see him earlier is because of his shielding. Two other guys linger near the trunk of the sedan, their faces masked in darkness, and a new level of rage boils every drop of blood inside me.

Fucking gofer-cronies.

Suddenly, the thing I overheard Holland say to Kylie inside the rink—*the private event thing on Friday*—hits differently. *This isn't curiosity—this is a test.* A practice run for the main event.

My body buzzes as I push myself into her space both mentally and physically, eating at the asphalt between us two stride-lengths at a time.

She sees the tire for the first time as she's unlocking her door, and confusion and panic render her body motionless. Holland is fast, but I'm faster as I dominate the space in front of her, crouching at the tire.

"Oh my God!" She jumps at my unexpected presence, and her hand grasps at air, trying to hold and slow the rapid breath in her chest. The space between us fills with warm fog from the extra exhalation, and her pulse thrums noticeably in her trim neck.

My mouth waters. Much like pheromones, her blood calls to me.

I avert my eyes from the tempting vibration and pretend to inspect her tire that I don't need to inspect at all. I already know who and how and why.

"You've got a flat."

"W-where did you come from?" she asks, her voice squeaking. "Why are you here?"

I don't answer.

If I explain why I'm here, I don't get to stay quiet—and quiet is the only thing keeping this from turning into something that draws attention.

I run my fingers along the rubber, finding the puncture I already spotted across the parking lot. It's small and clean and deliberate. *Straight from a blade, not bad luck.*

My jaw tightens. "It's definitely flat," I say, forcing my voice to stay even. "You're going to need a spare."

"That's so weird," she says. "It was fine when I parked."

Yes, it was fine until it wasn't, because someone made it that way.

Holland and his goons are close by now; I can feel their presence behind me.

"What's going on? Everything okay?" Holland asks, voice smooth in the way that's meant to remind me of our disparity in rank and polite to make Kylie feel like his presence is one of comfort and care.

Kylie turns toward him, understandably confused about where we've all come from. "I think I've got a flat."

"No kidding," he says, stepping closer. "That's rough. It's pretty late, Kylie. You want me to give you a ride home?"

There it is. *Comfort and care and concern.* A certified knight in shining armor. Too bad she can't see his fucking fangs.

"That's really sweet of you, Holland, but I can't leave my car here all night. I need it for work in the morning."

"I'll call one of my guys," Holland offers, completely ignoring my presence. "He'll get it fixed and make sure it's in your driveway by sunrise."

I straighten slowly—primarily for Kylie's benefit so I don't frighten her more than she already is—standing and letting my six-foot-six frame tower over his much smaller one as I position myself between them.

"I've got it," I say. "Changing to the spare won't take more than ten minutes."

Holland's smile tightens. His gaze searches my face, disdain and irritation bristling in the depths of his cold, dead eyes, but I don't budge.

Try me, you piece of shit. I'll tear your fucking head off.

Eventually, he looks back to Kylie with a refined smile plastered across his lips, undoubtedly aimed at broadening the gap between our personalities to win the tug-of-war on Kylie's instincts.

He's soft and I'm hard, he's nice and I'm short-tempered, he's rich and I'm poor. Anything to stack the deck in his favor.

"You sure?" he asks her. "Ten minutes seems like an eternity when you're freezing in the cold. It wouldn't be a problem at all to give you a lift, Kylie. Really. I'd be happy to do it."

"I said I've got it," I repeat. "If she's cold, she can wait in the car or the rink."

For a split second, something sharp flashes in his eyes, but just as quick as it came, it disappears, relegating me to the category of a simple nuisance. He doesn't see me as a real threat, and that's his biggest mistake of all.

Kylie blinks between us until her eyes settle on me. She doesn't understand why, but she trusts me more than him, regardless of the seemingly numerous reasons not to.

"Well…thank you, Rook. The spare would be great. Much more convenient in the end, I think. And thanks for the offer, Holland. Truly. It's kind of you."

I'm fucking proud of her for following her intuition.

Holland rocks back on his heels, glancing briefly at his guys before looking at me again. An inaudible sneer escapes his throat, but I ignore it.

"Well, Kylie," he says, his voice light now, "keep me in mind for Friday, okay?"

She nods. "Oh yeah. Of course. I'll let you know."

"See you around."

His buddies stare at me as they back away, their wordless expressions meant to put me on edge. Joke's on them, though. If anyone should be on edge right now, it's them.

There's no telling what I'd do to put myself between them and Kylie at this point, whether I'm ready for the commitment or not.

I wait until Holland and his cronies are gone before grabbing a jack from my truck.

Kylie crouches beside me, arms wrapped around herself against the cold when I kneel down to change her tire.

"I swear I'm not this helpless," she mutters. I don't know if it's more for her or for me, but the statement is emphatically loaded. Being something other than a damsel is important to her—in her eyes or mine, I'm not sure.

"You're not helpless," I confirm as kindly as I can manage while working on the flat.

It's only when she gasps in surprise at the ease with which I remove the tire without even using my fucking jack that I realize how mindlessly I'm going through the motions.

Idiot.

"So, you're, like, really strong."

I don't answer again because there isn't a good one. Not when she's vulnerable here, not when a simple explanation on my end would flip her entire world upside down.

Instead, I keep working, and muscle memory takes over while my mind tracks the lot. I don't miss that Holland and his lapdogs are still nearby in their sedan—just out of eyeshot but close enough to smell them—and I also don't miss the dark SUV idling across the street.

They're rushing because they need to. I fucking hate that I know why.

Kylie doesn't have a fucking clue what future is soon to befall her. She doesn't know what we are—what we're capable of. She doesn't know that she's *valuable.*

She doesn't know anything at all.

They must be desperate to lock her in before it's too late, because I know for a fact the main event isn't due to start for a few more weeks. With a woman who knows the rules? They can take it down to the wire.

With Kylie? They can't chance it.

"So…why do you…hate me?"

Her question comes out of thin fucking air and renders me temporarily motionless. I hold the spare up in front of the lugs, floating in frozen repose.

"What?"

"I know you don't like me. I mean, it's pretty *obvious*, you know? The part I can't seem to figure out is the *why*."

I can feel the intensity in my eyes as my head jerks toward hers. Nervously, she looks away and down at the pavement between us. And for the first time since every fucked-up cell inside my body decided to pick *her*, I wish she wouldn't.

"You always look like you're mad when I'm around," she adds quietly. "Doesn't take a genius to figure out I'm not your favorite person, but it might help if I knew why. If I offended you at some point or…I don't know…maybe you just find me annoying or something."

For an instant, my brain stings in revolt. *To have the other half of my whole believing I hate her is an assault against every one of my senses.*

I straighten slowly, turning back to the work to revive some of her comfort and putting the spare tire in place—this time remembering to use the jack for show. "I don't hate you, Kylie." My voice is raw with earnestness.

Fuck me, if you only knew what I actually feel for you, you'd be frightened for a whole other reason.

"Could've fooled me." She lets out a small, humorless laugh. "I don't think I've ever seen you smile."

I tighten the last bolt harder than necessary. "Well, that's probably because I hate *everyone*."

That earns me a look. A skeptical one.

"Wow. That's so…comforting," she says dryly.

Fuck, Rook. This is really going well. Clearly, I need to make sure she gets home safely and then get some distance from her before I can say any more stupid shit.

"All set." I lower the jack and stand, brushing my hands off on my jeans.

"That was…insanely fast," she says, marveling down at the spare tire that's now in place. "Thank you."

"Any time." I almost walk away, but I can't. Not without cautioning her more—not without leaving her with some impression of me other than disapproval and apathy.

I care. *The problem is, I care way too fucking much.*

"I know you're good and kind and friendly. But the rest of the world isn't as benevolent as it seems."

"Huh?" Her brow furrows. "What's the supposed to mean?"

"It means to trust your instincts. They were spot-on tonight. Keep listening to them and, more than anything else, avoid him."

"Avoid who?"

My eyes hold hers and my voice softens. It's perhaps the gentlest I've ever let myself sound toward her, and it's all because I want her to listen—to me, to herself, to all of it. "You know exactly who I mean."

She hesitates, assessing me carefully before agreeing. "Okay." I can't decide if she's taking me seriously or filing it away under *Rook being weird again*, but I have to hope this thing between us stacks the deck for the first.

I glance down and meet her gaze, desperate to get an inkling of where her mind is at right now.

The blue of her eyes is sharper than I remember, curiosity sending a zing of glitter through the deep pools of iris.

Women who know what's coming learn how to dull their eyes on command—to stow their emotions behind a veil. That's how I know without a shadow of a doubt that Kylie Moon has no idea what's on the horizon.

Her soul is wide open.

Turning abruptly, I head over to my truck to toss the flat tire and jack inside the bed. Every step feels like I'm wading through mud. My body, much to my chagrin, has absolutely no clue why I'm getting farther away from her.

When I return, she's got her passenger door open, rooting around in her skate bag. Holland's presence still pulses, heightening my anxiousness enough to hurry her along. "Now's not the time to reorganize your shit. It's time for you to get home. Don't stop anywhere."

Her brows knit, both in affront and confusion. "Ah, yes. An ominous command. I love those."

I sigh, forcing myself to stop being such a dick unintentionally. "It's late. It's dark. I'm concerned. That's all."

"Well, thanks, I guess."

I move to her car and open the driver's side door, holding it open for her and silently gesturing for her to get her ass inside. She stares at me for a long moment before a small laugh bubbles up. "Well, alrighty then. Going home it is."

I wait in silence as she climbs inside the car and tucks herself in with a click of her seat belt. When I shut the door, she rolls down the window.

"Thanks, Rook. I…appreciate the help."

She says my name like it means something, and my body responds like it believes her, every nerve going taut from head to toe.

"You're welcome." I nod. But I also really want her to get out of this fucking parking lot and somewhere safe. "Straight home, remember?"

She laughs, starting the engine with a nod, rolling up her window, and heading out of the rink parking lot while I watch.

The SUV is gone. The sedan is gone. But that doesn't change the reality that they tried to isolate her, and they'll do it again.

Tonight's offer to drive her home. Friday's event invitation. They both left room for a no, but soon, they won't take no for an answer.

I climb into my truck and sit there longer than I should with my hands tight on the wheel. I tell myself I'm not going to cross the line. I tell myself I'm not going to get involved.

But when I pull out my phone and look at the list in my notes app…

Flat Tire

Private Event

I know I'm lying.

5

Kylie

I AWAKEN HARSHLY TO THE SOUND OF A GARBAGE can banging into the ground and bolt straight up to sitting in bed. The numbers on my alarm clock taunt an hour that rubs—six a.m., and precisely thirty minutes before my usual wake-up—so bad it hurts.

The sheet is creased into both my arms like I slept motionless, and a crust of mouth-breathing drool tugs at the corner of my lips.

Lovely.

I scrub at my face with the sheet—one I'm washing tomorrow anyway—then mash my palms into my eyelids like I can physically shove the exhaustion back where it came from. I'm so worn thin lately, it's starting to feel like I work for a prison warden—

Another bang ricochets against my window, and I rocket-launch out of bed.

Shit, shit, shit, I forgot to put the can at the street last night!

I take off like the roadrunner in a blur of legs and arms throughout the otherwise quiet house.

Destination: garage.

I slide on bare feet as I round the corner of the hall, unlocking and ripping open the door at warp speed and leaning out to hit the opener. Alyssa is a dead sleeper, thank God, or she'd be running out here with her brother's pellet gun she keeps under her pillow and lighting me up in her sleep-infused haze *or* questioning, for the thousandth time, why in the hell I can never remember to put the damn trash at the street—a roommate-agreed-upon job of *mine*.

I jump down three steps without taking a single one of them, jarring my knee when I hit the cold concrete floor, and working swiftly to recover as I run and duck at the same time, sliding under the still-lifting panels.

On a mission, I stumble out from under the door on fawn-like legs that are nowhere near ready for this level of athleticism and lose what little fraction of control I had left. I bob and weave and trip and career, the frightening hard surface of the driveway coming toward my face in a terrifying rush.

Oh hell! I'm going to eat concrete in about two seconds.

But at the last moment, I run into a wall of hard muscle and leather gloves.

Rook's leather-covered hands set me back to vertical slowly, his eyes falling to my barely covered chest with unconcealed interest.

I follow his gaze and silently gasp. An unswallowable knot grows in my throat as I realize I was so tired last night, I went to bed in nothing but boy shorts and my lace bra—an outfit I'm still sporting right now.

"Oh my God," I whisper, mortification making itself known in the heat of my face. Instantly, I try to shield my lace-covered boobs by crossing my arms over my chest, but it's freaking useless. If anything, it's only making the situation more…*booby.*

Rook's jaw tightens like he's fighting a battle he didn't ask for.

"Sorry, um…" *God help me. This is so awkward.* "I woke up approximately sixty seconds ago to the unfortunate realization that I forgot to bring down my can. I know I'm a thorn in your side with this thing every dang week."

"I know." His voice is gruff when he responds, and his eyes look like smoke and haze as he works to lift them from my spilling breasts. It's a battle he nearly loses in every facet, and for the first time in a while, I feel a joyful twinge at being ogled. "I was getting it for you."

The admission is so surprisingly friendly, I startle. "You were…you were getting my can for me?"

"You always have a full can." His voice is rough and heavy with something severe. "Another week without garbage pickup, and the whole neighborhood would stink."

I deflate a little, disappointed that we're back to brusque, judgmental Rook this quickly. I know it's naïve, but I really hoped he'd made some progress last night toward not hating me so much.

"Well, thanks, I guess." I swallow, trying to act normal while I'm basically in lingerie on my driveway. "I'll really try to remember to put it out Monday night next time."

His strong shoulders sag slightly, almost as though he's disappointed in my response. I don't know why—I'm being perfectly friendly.

And still, I don't understand him.

I wish I could see inside his head for just a second so I could know whether I'm imagining all this tension or if it's actually there.

Because if I am, I'd really like to stop tripping over it or, you know, procure an invisibility cloak from Harry Potter and make myself disappear whenever he's around.

Or, hell, maybe it'd be easier if he could see inside *my* head.

If he could hear what I'm thinking, then he'd understand that I'm not trying to make his job harder. I'm not doing the trash-can sprint every week to be annoying; I'm just tired and scattered and trying not to fall apart at the seams.

He'd see that I don't have anything against him.

If anything, I wish I could get to know you better, my mind whispers.

And I almost say it.

I open my mouth, but then I quickly smash my lips shut.

Some things are probably better left in my head.

6

ROOK

YLIE'S ARMS CROSS TIGHTER OVER HER VO-luptuous chest, and her knees turn inward against the cold as she looks at me like she's waiting for something I don't know how to give.

I look everywhere but at her.

Because if I don't, I'm going to do something reckless—like pull her against me, sink my teeth into the steady thrum at her neck, and lose myself in the way our bodies would fit together if I let them.

Every minute—every fucking second—the pressure in my chest grows heavier. It isn't desire alone. It's overwhelming need. And it's sharp and constant and feels like something pressing against every cell inside my body.

Just last month, I was a man with his own boundaries. His own decisions. His own rules. Now, it feels like something is leaning on me from the inside, testing every single thing I thought I knew. Like my body and mind and cold heart are trying to morph into a vessel for something that is far greater than me.

Even this morning, getting out of the truck to grab her

forgotten can wasn't a choice. It was a pull. One I didn't bother fighting because I didn't think it mattered.

And fuck, the pull is only growing stronger now. The need to just be *close* to her is fucking with my head.

To make things worse, I can smell *him* here—feel his intentions in the wood of the siding and the pores of the concrete beneath us—and every destructive part of me begs to be unleashed. To hunt him. To kill him. To burn the entire damn roster of the Fighting Fangs alive if I have to.

Because if I can feel him like this, that means he was here last night.

This morning, maybe.

That means he's getting desperate enough to take chances, and when a man like Holland Thorne is cornered—his whole spoon-fed life on the line—he'll do dangerous things.

Why? Why can't he look me in the eye?

The thought cuts through the noise like it doesn't belong to me.

It's like there's a wall between us, and if I could just chip away at the top few bricks, I'd be able to see him better.

I stiffen.

Those thoughts aren't mine. But they're sliding through my mind slowly, unfamiliar in texture and weighted with emotion that doesn't originate in my body. And yet, somehow, they feel far more personal than those I hear in visions or from other people's minds when they willingly open them up to me.

Why do I want him to look at me so badly? Why do I want him to favor me? To be soft with me? Why does it bother me so much that Rook Slater hates me? Why—

Realization overwhelms me in a jolt, and I startle, my eyes jumping to Kylie's ocean-blue gaze and holding. I'm hearing *her*. *Her thoughts, her worries, her insecurities about* me…

Fuck. I shouldn't be able to do this. I don't know why I can do this. *Yes, you fucking do. You know exactly why,* my own mind screams at me.

Though, Kylie's thoughts practically overpower it. *I just don't get why he hates me so much.*

This feels *wrong.* And way too invasive.

I clear my throat, struggling to block out any and all other thoughts while simultaneously setting her mind at ease. To somehow, without exposing myself to a total surrender of control, convey that I don't hate her. "Kylie, I'm…sorry. For the way I am with you. It's not…personal. Really. I find you…quite tolerable."

"Quite tolerable?" Her giggle shocks me. "Well, thanks, Rook," she says, now smiling at me. "I think you're pretty *tolerable* too. Especially when you're saving me from trash purgatory for another week and fixing my flats in the dark, cold, late night. The past twenty-four hours are really advancing your bid for the knight in shining armor position in my life."

The corner of my mouth lifts before I can stop it.

And the ache in my chest eases just a bit.

"I should get back to my route," I say, even though every part of me wants to stay exactly where I am.

"Of course," she says, bouncing to ward off the cold, while a blush steals the peach of her cheeks and replaces it with red. "I have to get to work too."

"Bye, Kylie," I allow myself to say, the satisfaction of her name on my tongue giving temporary aid to my ongoing chest pain.

"Goodbye, Rook."

She backs into her garage, and I turn to make the lonely walk back to my truck. When I climb inside, the garage door has closed, and the pain is back with full force. If vampires were susceptible to heart attacks, I surely would've already kicked the bucket.

I grit my teeth against the urge to sit there—to escort her to work, to the rink, and back home again like some kind of guard dog she never asked for—and force my attention forward.

I know where that road leads. I know the fight waiting at the end of it. And I know the danger it puts her in, the danger it puts my brothers in.

I know the fallout won't just stop with me.

If I give in to what's pulling me—if I stop pushing back against the current between us—*everything* changes.

But the truth I keep circling is simpler than all of that.

Protecting her isn't something I chose.

It's something I can't *not* do.

I'd burn everything to the fucking ground just to keep her safe.

1

KYLIE

*I*T'S ONLY TUESDAY, BUT IT FEELS LIKE IT SHOULD be Friday.

Between the flat tire last night, sprinting outside this morning in my underwear, and the fact that Rook Slater has somehow lodged himself firmly in my head, I'm already running on fumes—and my workday has barely started.

Add in four thousand tasks that appeared on my to-do list overnight, and I'm hanging on by a thread.

Thankfully, I'm not the only one suffering. Martin looks like he's one deduction question away from an orange jumpsuit, and because misery loves company, I appreciate the solidarity.

Sighing heavily, I work through crossed eyes to make sense of a return that stopped making sense an hour ago, and I fight an earnest battle not to look at the clock again.

There's no point—I know that—because it only makes the spreadsheets feel worse and the time feel longer, but old habits die hard when you're a glutton for punishment. The last time I reset the metaphorical whiteboard with *minutes since last loss of willpower,* it was six thirty, and upon stupid inspection now, it's six thirty-two.

God help me. This day is the equivalent of eternity.

My phone buzzes on a stack of manila folders, and I dive to answer it, eager for any and all respite.

And you thought it might be Rook for some reason too.

Of course, it's not him—I don't even think he has my number, *and* I'm clearly losing my marbles to even think *he'd* be calling *me*—but my grandmother instead.

"Hey, Gammy."

"Pot roast is in the slow cooker. Should be done in about an hour."

There's no preamble on her end, and because I'm a walking zombie, my mistake doesn't click without the full reminder.

"I also made a batch of my biscuits you love so much. What time do you think you'll be here?"

Shit. I completely forgot about the serious-talk pot roast and the refusal to take no for an answer. I meant to call her during my lunch break today, but I never got a lunch break. Maybe I'd have remembered this morning if Rook hadn't thrown off my whole morning routine too, but between him and taxes, I barely have two brain cells to rub together.

The *thought* of driving the forty-five minutes to her house, having dinner, and back again is nearly enough to break me. I can't imagine how it'd feel in practice.

"Gammy, I'm so, so sorry I didn't get in touch earlier, but I can't tonight." I cringe. "I'm still at work, and there are no signs of leaving thus far."

Silence consumes the line and bleeds out onto my shoulders,

doing one hell of an impression of a twenty-pound set of dumbbells. I feel awful, but feeling awful is better than feeling dead. At least, I think.

"You've been working late a lot," Gammy eventually says. "Maybe a little too much, sweetheart."

"Yeah, well, it's tax season."

"I know when tax season is," she replies with the well-earned authority of a woman who's lived through eighty tax seasons. "I also know when my granddaughter sounds worn so thin her priorities have started to jumble."

I rub my temple, searching for an olive branch I can handle. "I promise I'll come out this weekend for dinner. How about Saturday night? I'll make sure my whole schedule is clear just for you. Maybe I'll even sleep there."

She pauses for a long moment. "All right, dear. I wish it were sooner, but Saturday will have to do, I guess. Everything else okay?"

"Yes," I say automatically.

"And the people around you?" she asks. "How are they?"

My fingers still on the keyboard as my brow furrows in confusion. *What is she talking about? Why the hell does she care how anyone else is feeling?*

I'm too tired to question it aloud. Instead, I do my best to answer. "They're fine, I guess. Alyssa is busy with school, and she's the only one I really—"

"No, no, dear. I meant how are they...*with you?*"

"Gammy, not going to lie, you've been a little heavy on weird questions lately and very cryptic on the need to speak in person. I don't get it. Did you get intel from the CIA about a sleeper cell in Concordia or something? Are *you* CIA? Make it make sense, please, and do it slowly, like you're talking to a child."

"I just like to know that my girl is safe," she says with a sigh. "That's all."

"Well, you don't need to be worried," I reassure. "I'm fine. I promise. My life consists of work, skate, and sleep. And every once in a while, I reward myself with a cube of cheese." I offer a small laugh. One I hope puts her at ease since *The Devil Wears Prada* is one of her favorite movies.

It doesn't work, though, her gloomy mood persisting through a soft hum of disapproval. "And what about men? Any gentlemen suitors trying to grab your attention?"

"*Gentlemen suitors?* Come on, Gammy." I snort. "Your age is showing."

"I just want to know if there's a new man in your life, sweetheart. Someone trying to be helpful, perhaps?"

Helpful. The word lands strangely.

I think of the flat tire last night and the way Rook Slater came to my rescue and changed it with such ease and speed, it felt superhuman. Along with the trash can this morning, his attention to rescuing me is compounding at an exponential rate.

Putting it to Gammy like that seems like an exercise in my own torture, though, and with Martin now standing in the door of his office, waving at me like he's floating in the ocean waiting for a life preserver, I don't think complicating this conversation is in my best interest.

Keep it simple.

"I did have a flat last night at the rink," I answer. "One of the guys who plays hockey there helped me. But that was it, and I've known him for quite a while."

Known him to be grumpy and standoffish, but known him all the same.

Gammy goes quiet, and Martin's arms turn manic. I hold up a hand and pump my palm toward him three times to suggest he cool his fucking jets.

"You got a flat tire in the middle of the night?" Gammy questions shakily. "That doesn't sound safe, Kylie."

"The flat tire wasn't safe, but the guy who changed it was." *I think.* "It was no big deal."

"No big deal? Sounds like a recipe to end up with your face on a missing persons poster to me."

"Maybe another time," I say in a gentle tease. "This time, it led me right back to work for another twelve-hour day."

"Just be careful, Kylie, okay?" She snaps back. "The rest of the world isn't as benevolent as it seems. There are men out there who would hurt you. Who would take advantage of your looks and your kindness in ways you don't like."

The rest of the world isn't as benevolent as it seems.

Those are Rook's same words from last night, making it the second time I've heard the unusual warning in twenty-four hours after never hearing it before in my entire life. It's unsettling, to say the least. My eyes unfocus, and the hair on my arms stands on end.

"Gammy, I promise I'm always careful."

"That's what your mother used to say too."

It's been years since Gammy has brought something up about my mother or her and my father's tragic deaths that left me orphaned at a young age. She's done her best to shield me from the truth—that they were murdered in cold blood—but this is a 180-degree reversal if I've ever seen one.

She's not just mentioning it. She's using it to emotionally manipulate me.

"Gammy." My chest tightens. "That's not fair, and you know it."

"I know," she says softly. "I know it's not fair, but neither is life, sweetheart. You're important to me. I love you. And if reminding you of the stakes of this world saves my granddaughter from harm, I'll do it until I'm blue in the face."

"I love you too," I reply, and mean it to my freaking bones. My gammy is the world to me, but I can't say this call has left me feeling anything other than worse for wear.

I'm tired. Worn thin. Anxious. And now I can add downright terrified to the list.

"You give me a call later this week so we can make plans for Saturday," she orders. "Don't back out on me, you hear? I'll stalk you if I have to."

"You could tell me the important things now, you know? Break the suspense."

"No, honey, unfortunately, I can't," she responds, not giving a single inch of explanation. "See you Saturday. I'll make chicken potpie."

Before I can say anything, the line goes dead, and like a two-for-one special, Martin is now standing directly over my desk.

I'd have loved a moment to muddle through the emotions my grandmother left me with, but evidently, that level of self-care will have to wait.

"Oh, thank God, I thought you'd never get off the phone. I

need the Fred Howard return again. He *found* some more income in his *other* bank account." He rolls his eyes. "So now he needs me to *find* some more expenses."

I snort, and he laughs.

"Yeah, that's what I said. According to him, I keep a stockpile shoved up my ass." He sighs. "Whatever. I just need to correct the income, and then you can file. We'll deal with his upset later."

"Ten-four. I'll send it back to you now."

Martin nods and retreats to his office, and I yawn into my free hand while I wield the mouse in the other. By the time Fred Howard's business return is finalized and sent to his email—thirty minutes later—Martin and I are the only ones left.

I scream out to announce my departure, and he moans in reply. I don't bother inquiring on his well-being any further—I've got myself to worry about.

It's dark outside and my brain is fried, and no matter how much I wish I had the energy to go skate, I know with every ounce of my being that carbs and trashy reality TV is the only cure to this level of walking-carcass.

I hop into my Civic and start the engine, rubbing at my hands as the evening cold makes the heat struggle to get going. Giving the old girl a minute to warm up, I pick up my phone out of the cupholder with the urge to scroll, and a message appears on the screen.

> Unknown: Hey, Kylie. It's Holland from the rink. Hope it's okay I got your number from Ted, but after you got that flat last night, it felt imperative that you have my number just in case you find yourself in a bind again.

Ted is the general manager of the rink, and as much as I'd love to believe he thought the action was harmless, it was a big error of judgment to give out my phone number to someone without asking.

Holland's always been nice to me, but Rook, for all his eccentricities, seems to hate him far more than he hates everyone else.

Oh well. It's not like Holland having my number is the key to my safe-deposit box or a straight line to my Social Security number. If things get dicey, I can always change the number— *thanks to my grandmother, I'm quite familiar with the process.*

> **Me: Please don't jinx me with another flat tire.**

Three dots appear almost immediately.

> **Holland: Ha. Promise I'm not trying to do that. How's the tire holding up, by the way? That dude Rook get it handled?**

Rook's deep, mysterious brown eyes fill my mind, and a weird urge to push Holland's buttons as a test overwhelms me. *Is the distrust mutual? Or is Rook just being…well, Rook?*

> **Me: Holding up well. Rook got it fixed in no time at all. He was great, actually.**

> **Holland: Glad to hear it. Listen, about that thing on Friday I mentioned. I don't want to pressure you to do anything you don't want to do, but I do think it's a great opportunity. There are a lot of talent scouts looking for beautiful, talented women like you for modeling shoots, commercials, etc.**

Before I can overthink it, another message comes through.

Holland: All I'm saying is to keep an open mind about it, okay?

This whole private event thing on Friday night is his favorite topic of conversation, to say the least. I mean, I still don't even know what it entails, but it's clear he wants me to go. He didn't react to the Rook comment, but maybe the desperation to come to his thing *is* a reaction?

I exhale, longing for a time when the men were just staring at me, and send the most appropriate response.

Me: Okay.

It's a pathetically bland reply, but right now, at the end of a marathon run of swirling emotions, inconveniences, and piles and piles of work on broken, bleeding feet, it's all I have to give.

I toss my phone into the cupholder and head toward my favorite takeout place—Murray's Pub—to drown my exhaustion in grease. Fried chicken, a burger, potato skins—it all sounds good. *I think I'll order it all and welcome the indigestion as the antidote to overthinking.*

The lot is half full when I pull in, most of the spaces filled by expensive black cars and SUVs. It's not commonplace per se, but the greater Boston area is far wealthier than most people realize. I have an inside track because of my everyday work digging through their financials, but I'm still a little surprised to find them here, slumming it with the commonfolk.

Bleeping my locks, I smile to myself about the suited crowd I'm bound to find inside, and ready myself for several encounters with the same personality.

Miss, where's my order? I said on the side, not on the top! I've been waiting for ten minutes, for God's sake!

The bell chimes over my head as I step inside the neon-sign-adorned lobby area, dusting the gravel off my boots on the black rubber mat. I push my hair out of my face and unbutton my coat, weaving through a crowd of people waiting for a table and heading straight for the counter to put in my to-go order.

The clientele is exactly as I expected—though pretty overtly male in an angering sort of way—and I shake my head at the feminist voice inside my head. *Maybe it's not that women aren't wealthy too—they're just eating somewhere that doesn't clog their arteries quite as quickly.*

I focus on Gemma, my favorite do-it-all gal behind the counter, willing her to come to me with her little pad and pencil and leave all these other people to fend for themselves.

"Well, hey there," a familiar voice says from my side. "Small world."

Holland's smile is both edgy and surprised, and my heart gallops violently in my chest. We were literally just texting five freaking minutes ago, and now, he's here. At one of my favorite places.

He looks just as surprised to see me as I am him, but still, an uneasiness that doesn't even feel like my own washes over me until I'm shivering.

"Apparently," I reply, forcing a smile.

"Listen, since we're both—"

A rush of cold outside air hits me in the back so hard it's as though the front door is right behind me. Holland is still talking as I turn around, but I don't even hear him as my eyes land on

Rook Slater without any effort at all. A dozen bodies fill the space by the entrance, and yet, his face stands out instantly.

It's intense and unforgiving in ways I can't fully comprehend as he stares at the man to my left.

Behind Rook, his brother Kane eases the mood with a friendly smile, grasping Rook's shoulder and shaking it as if to loosen him. Rook's laser focus finally breaks, and without hesitation, his eyes jump to me. His body moves, Kane seemingly prancing behind him in comparison to his stern steps, and I find myself bracing for impact.

Last night's flat tire commune was intense; this looks primed to be worse. Keys dangle from Kane's fingers, and when our eyes meet, he grins at me, which, thankfully, settles some of my nerves.

"Hey, Kylie," he says easily, nudging Rook to the side so they can stand shoulder to shoulder, by and large ignoring the hockey adversary at my side. "Just the woman we were looking for."

"Uh…hi." I pause, glancing between Kane and Rook, as they confirm that their being here, as opposed to Holland, isn't a coincidence at all. "Wait…what do you mean *looking for?*"

Rook's gaze flicks to the keys in my hand before moving to my eyes and holding. I feel trapped there, and I'm surprisingly comfortable in the confinement. He should scare me much more than he does—logically, I know that—but intrinsically, I always feel…*safe* when he's nearby.

"Your spare's temporary," he says. "Not quite full size. We need to switch it out with a standard wheel."

"But my car is working fine. I drove it to work this morning without any issues."

"I know," he says. "But it's temporary."

"I can't even tell the difference," I say, glancing at Kane.

Kane laughs. "I like you, Kylie. It's always nice for us men when we meet a woman where size truly doesn't matter."

I snort despite myself, and Rook hits him with a glare so lethal I'm surprised the whole establishment doesn't quake.

"I know it's not the most convenient when you just want to get your food and go home," Kane adds. "But my tow's out front. Will only take five minutes, tops."

"Your tow?" I question. I know Kane is like the local Repo Man of Concordia, but I don't understand why my car needs a tow when it's running just fine.

"Just to be safe," Kane reassures. "Wouldn't want that tire falling off before we get it switched out."

"My tire falling off?" I question, my eyes going wide in shock. "That's a thing that can happen?'

"No," Holland chimes in on a scoff at the same time Kane says, "Yes."

"No one asked you for your opinion," Rook snaps, but his eyes never leave my face. "Just let me get it switched out for you, Kylie. Otherwise, it's going to drive me crazy, thinking something bad could happen."

I look to Holland warily. His smile is tight, but his eyes are sharply focused on Rook, his posture locked in place. I can't stop myself from glancing back at Rook, but I startle when I find his eyes are still on me.

I've seen the violent way these guys slam each other on the ice whenever they get a chance—the sin bin has yet to be empty during their games—but this beef between them feels meatier than some hockey grudge. In fact, it feels *uncomfortably* tied to me, and I can't for the life of me figure out why.

"Uh…" I pause, my eyes still bouncing around the three guys like a ping-pong ball. I'm tired. And hungry. And my nerves are so fucking shot it's not funny.

I don't know what to do here to make the feelings go away. *And I really, really need the feelings to go away.*

"How about I just have one of my guys look at it for you, Kylie?" Holland offers. "You can get your food, and I can give you a lift home."

Rook tenses, but Kane cuts in with a laugh. "Holland, bud, I think we can all agree that your guys don't know their asshole from a screwdriver. Comparatively, Cal's the best mechanic in Concordia. I say we let my brother handle it, yeah?"

"Best mechanic?" Holland scoffs. "I thought he was the scrub who did demo work."

"Demolition shit is his side hustle," Kane corrects.

"His side hustle?" Holland's eyebrows pinch together, and Kane just laughs.

"Oh, my bad. I forgot not all of us have been sucking off the golden teat since birth," Kane says through another laugh that's far more sarcastic than anything else. "Side hustle is like a second job."

"I know what a side hustle is," Holland comments with a roll of his eyes. "I just didn't realize Calloway was a mechanic."

"Mechanic by day." Kane winks. "Demolition man by night."

Holland is silent after that, but his tight jaw says enough. He's fucking pissed at the golden teat jab, and the stakes I thought were high before have only been elevated.

"Dinner's on us, Kylie," Kane cuts in, and before I know it, he's wrapping a friendly arm around my shoulders. "Put your order in, and we'll have your tire changed out and you back here before your food's ready."

"It's really going to be that quick?"

"Five minutes, tops," Rook answers. "You don't even have to get out of Kane's tow truck."

"Why don't I just wait here, then?"

"Sorry, Kylie." Kane pretends to wince. "Need you to sign on both ends of the tow. But I promise it'll be quick, and I'll even let you choose our music selection." Kane punctuates the promise with a waggle of his brows.

Holland's intensity at my side is enough to make me agree. "Okay, fine. But I better not end up with cold takeout." I have a feeling if I push, he'll be volunteering to hang out with me while I wait, and for some reason, that makes me feel shaky.

"Thanks for the offer, Holland, but don't worry about me. Don't delay your dinner any more than you already have."

"All right," he agrees. A perfectly friendly smile is plastered across his lips, but it feels as fake as my press-on nails. "I'll see you around, Kylie."

"Hey, Ky. Sorry it took me so long tonight," Gemma comments as if summoned. "What can I get you?"

I turn to offer Holland the opportunity to order first, but he's already out the door, no food in sight.

My brow wrinkles as I turn back to Gemma, Rook and Kane standing sentry at my side. "Oh, uh…no problem. I'll have the skins, the burger with tomato, pickle, lettuce, and no onion, and, what the hell…give me an order of the fried wings too."

Glancing over my shoulder, I do my best to bring this

interaction with the intense hockey brigade back to some level of normalcy. "You guys want something? I can put it in with my order."

Kane looks primed to answer, but Rook beats him to it. "No. Thanks."

I shrug, turning back to Gemma. "That's all, I guess. But hey, I have to run a quick errand with these guys, so if I'm not back yet when it's up, you mind leaving it under the warmer?"

Gemma smiles. "No problem."

"Thanks, girl."

Kane leads the way out the door, and Rook waits to follow me from behind. I can feel his eyes on me the whole way, but I don't dare look back or say anything. Everything with him feels so pointedly precarious.

When we get to the parking lot, most of the fancy cars are gone, even though the majority of the patrons inside are still there, and an eerie feeling blows across me like the wind.

Rook steps around me and holds out a hand, cutting the feeling mysteriously short. "Keys?"

"She's all yours," I say, dropping them into his hand with care. Our fingers just barely brush, and a consuming feeling runs through me, so intense my eyes water and my nose stings. I swallow hard and force a step back as he spins on harsh feet and gets to work.

I can't help but wonder if he feels it too. Or if all this stress and confusion have me truly losing a grasp on reality.

The tow truck lights blink as Kane guides my car onto the lift and secures the chains in no time at all. Rook helps me into the cab before climbing in himself, and Kane gets behind the wheel, officially putting me in a Slater brother sandwich for the ride.

If Alyssa were in my shoes, she'd be focused on finding a way to turn the close proximity into a three-way. *At the very least, talk one of them into licking her kitty or something.*

I literally feel my cheeks heat from the thought, and I discreetly glance at Kane and Rook, fearful that I did something crazy like say the words out loud. *Or, I don't know, that my previous wish came true, and Rook can read my freaking mind.*

But all I find is Kane smiling and nodding along to the song on the radio and Rook stone-faced and staring out the window.

Cal's garage is only a mile or two up the road, and I'm still surprised at how efficient they are as they get my car off the tow.

When I was sixteen and a brand-new driver, Gammy's car broke down on the highway, and I had to use AAA. It took the man *hours* to get there and hook it up, much less drive me to her house so her neighbor could fix it for her. Maybe he was obnoxiously slow, but the Slater brothers are exceptionally fast.

It's truly impressive watching them, and watching Rook, especially, is something else.

I observe from the cab through the rearview mirror as he unhooks my car and pushes it back into the bay, studying the parts of his body his grumpy face usually precludes me from. His hands are big and strong but finessed, and the muscles in his forearms are chiseled like tan stone. His white shirt is stained with use, and his hair drifts effortlessly onto the skin above his eyes.

He's not sweating, but even without a sheen, he emanates a surprising glow.

Cal smiles and waves a hello from the bay door before setting to work getting my car on the lift, and Rook returns to the door to take his spot as the hood disappears.

His posture is casual and his eyes averted to the inside of the garage, but I get the most unshakable feeling that he's taken up this position with the intention of keeping watch over me.

Barely five minutes have passed before my Civic is on its way back out the door while Cal wipes his hands on a red rag. Kane is first to climb back into the tow truck and graciously hands over a fresh coffee in a to-go mug.

"Figured you might need this."

"Thanks."

My body melts at the smell alone. I can't even imagine how good it's going to be when it hits my lips.

Rook's body startles mid-climb into the truck, his wide eyes jumping to my face and freezing. I blush under the scrutiny, all the while trying to maintain some sense of reality.

"What? What's wrong?"

He shakes his head to clear it but only after his jaw has tightened noticeably. When I turn back to Kane to thank him again, his eyebrows are raised dramatically.

"What?" I ask, repeating my question to him.

He shakes his head, firing up the engine. "Nothing, babe. And you're welcome for the coffee. Happy to help a woman in need at any time."

I laugh. "Do I look that tired?"

Kane winks. "A minute or two from collapse."

I sigh. "It's been a long week already, and it's barely even started."

Rook's throat-clearing is hard to miss. "Let's get you back

to Murray's, then, so you can get home." I would take offense, but I'm too busy noticing the way his jean-clad muscular thigh brushes mine.

Seriously, Ky. Stop it. The man is actively trying to get rid of you as we speak.

"What do I owe you?" I ask as Kane pulls out of the parking lot and accelerates toward the pub. "For the new tire," I add. "I know new tires aren't cheap."

"Nothing." Rook's voice brooks no argument, but the idea of letting them eat the cost of a whole freaking tire is absurd. They're blue-collar guys—just regular people like me. I cannot stand the thought of being the reason they're short on money this month.

"But I—"

"Don't even try," Kane cuts in with a laugh. "He won't change his mind. Rook's allergic to letting women pay for things."

I hate the intent focus my mind finds on the plural form of the word. *Women, not woman. And certainly not Kylie Moon, specifically.*

"Well, thanks," I say, forcing myself back onto safer ground. "Both of you."

When Kane pulls into Murray's Pub, he jerks a thumb toward his brother and digs me even further into the hole of gratitude. "Rook's paying for your order. Don't argue. It'll just make him grumpier."

I turn to Rook, my expression full of both question and thanks, and he rubs a hand through his hair, struggling to make eye contact as he agrees. "I'll come inside with you."

Kane claps, startling our attention off each other. "Great. I'll get your car off the truck while you guys get your food."

"I didn't—" I start, but Rook is already hopping out of the cab and heading toward the pub.

I follow him out of the truck, trying and failing to make him focus on me as he holds the door to Murray's, pays for my order, and hands me my bag of food.

He's so freaking hot and cold, he might as well be a menthol back patch.

What is with this guy?

Acknowledgment or not, though, I can still feel the heat of his fingers where they touched mine in the bag exchange ten minutes later. He's long gone, the bag of food he paid for in the passenger seat my only company, and yet, I feel as though he's still right freaking here all night long.

Sitting quietly at my side as I indulge in one too many heavy foods.

Grinding his jaw when a new message from Holland—making sure I made it home okay and reminding me about Friday—rolls in when I'm tucking into bed.

Staring at me as I sleep, even though the pillow on my bed is rounded, cold, and empty.

Alyssa isn't home, and yet, I feel wildly un-alone.

I can't shake the feeling that something is brewing beneath the surface of my life. And worse yet, I get the sense I'm not in control of it at all.

8

ROOK

THE WORST PART ABOUT KNOWING WHAT'S COMING is that nobody believes you enough to act until it's too late. Because everything looks the same—for now. Because the danger is theoretical—for now.

Because it's too much work and worry to imagine routine won't continue untouched.

Concordia is still Concordia. The roads still wind through pines and fog, and Murray's Pub still glows like an outsider on the corner of McMansion Street and Fuckoffwealth Way.

Vampires and humans alike live their lives like they aren't being rearranged by forces they don't even know exist.

But the shift is imminent anyway; I can feel it.

For years and years, vampires have been letting their mates be stolen out from under their noses by the elites and their gofers—all because of tradition. Because of entitlement from the top, and their assumed ownership over the three most potent human bloodlines, despite the universe's clear direction otherwise.

The *blood of the three* and the elites' need to hoard it wasn't on my top ten list to care about.

But now, the ritual continues with Kylie Moon.

The flat tire last night wasn't a question. The text messages today served a purpose. And Holland being at Murray's Pub tonight when Kylie was there was a calculated move.

And holy fuck, do I care.

I should be home relishing my woodworking hobby or losing myself in the mindless literature of eighteenth-century aristocrats, but because I can't get rid of the bow in my back or the knife in my chest, I'm here instead, trying to find the words to turn my brothers' worlds upside down.

Cal's garage is quiet at this time of night, save the buzz from the overhead lights and the faint thump of nineties hip-hop playing through the speakers. Tools hang on the wall all around, and the concrete below our feet reeks of oil and rubber and metal.

Kane pushes back from the old '69 Camaro we've been working on, wiping his hands on a rag and eyeing me closely. He can feel the pulse of my need to speak well before the words even form in my throat, as it's always been his gift to preemptively read intent.

Calloway leans against a workbench, arms crossed, watching me too. Their patience to stay quiet and wait for me to spit it out is waning, however, and Kane is the first to break it.

"You're spiraling," he says.

"I'm fine."

He barks a laugh. "You're never fine. You're just more or less homicidal, and right now, you're wielding six knives, four swords, and a guillotine."

I drag a hand down my jaw, forcing myself to find some

semblance of control as the text from Holland to Kylie he sent five minutes ago rolls around in my mind.

I shouldn't be able to sense what he says to her. Shouldn't be able to hear their conversations from afar or read his texts without being included in the chain. I shouldn't be able to hear her thoughts like I did this morning in her driveway—or like I did tonight as she thought sensuously about putting her lips to her coffee.

And yet…I can.

Hope you made it home okay, Kylie. And don't forget about Friday, okay? I'd really love to take you to the event.

The words sit in my head like a bruise I keep pressing just to see if it still hurts. They're dangerous—Holland is dangerous—and I know with an instinct I can't shake that time is running out.

"You're burning tracks in Cal's concrete," Kane says. "Just spit it out, bro. Say what you really want to say."

I stop pacing at once, my decision made. I can't stand by and let it happen. Not to her.

I won't.

And then, I say it. The three words that are an open door to chaos and change we won't come back from. The three words my brothers won't be able to ignore.

"They've chosen her."

Of course, the words land hard.

Kane paid witness to Holland's intention tonight, and Cal's heard the curiosity at the rink with his super hearing himself, but my saying this—putting this fine a point on the endgame—dials the stakes up to an eleven.

Calloway straightens. "You're sure?"

"Yes."

"How?" Cal asks. "We haven't been keeping an eye on Holland for that long. We haven't been—"

"I don't need long," I cut him off. "I don't need proof, Cal. I *know*."

Calloway's eyes narrow. "How?"

I drag a hand down my face. "Our…*pairing*. You know how it works."

"Technically, we *don't* know how it works," Kane interjects. "At least, not specifically. You're the first to fall to this particular fate, brother, so why don't you enlighten us?"

Fuck me. I shake my head. "I just *know*, okay?"

Kane's gaze sharpens. "You're tracking him."

"Tracking who?" Calloway asks. "Holland? He's just a gofer doing gofer things."

"No, Cal. He's a gofer who's circling," I correct. "And he doesn't circle unless he's told to. And right now, he's circling Kylie. So yes, I'm tracking him."

It's an admission steeped in a million brutal consequences. It doesn't matter if she's fated to me or that they're usurping our bond. *Our kind* isn't supposed to track *their kind*. It's not just illegal; it's a death sentence.

Kane lets out a low whistle. "Well, shit. I guess our stepping in tonight was a little more complicated than messing with a Fighting Fang, then, wasn't it?" He groans. "Blood of the fucking three, my dear holiness, we are so fucking far up shit's creek, it's not even funny."

"I didn't plan to put you in that position," I say. "I didn't plan any of it. To be honest, I didn't even realize I was doing it at first."

"How?" Calloway asks, defaulting into containment mode. "How are you tracking him? Is it traceable? Phone? GPS?"

I shake my head. "Nothing like that."

"Then how the hell do you know what he's saying to her?"

The answer isn't clean—and saying it out loud makes it worse. But clearly, we're long past keeping things to myself now. I've put us all in the crosshairs.

"I feel it," I admit sheepishly. "When he pushes. When she hesitates. When something shifts." I clear my throat. "I can hear her thoughts if I let myself, too. It's…like we're one instead of two."

The silence that follows is thick.

"Fuck me." Calloway exhales slowly. "You're…locked in."

Kane folds his arms. "You do realize what that means."

"Yes," I say, resigned to my own body's decisions.

"And you're doing it anyway."

"Yes."

Calloway steps closer. "We've never interfered in the elite's bullshit, Rook. No one has."

"I know."

"It's bullshit. It's always been bullshit. We all know that," Kane adds. "But once you step in, you don't step back out."

"I know," I say.

"Because once you take a woman off their board," Kane continues, "you're not just breaking etiquette. You're declaring war."

"I didn't choose this. I wouldn't have chosen this, and I don't think Kylie would have either. But it's happening."

Calloway's voice is careful. "She doesn't know?"

I turn away, staring at the concrete floor—at the dark stains where cars have leaked their insides to the point of extinction and then been brought back to life at my brother's hands. But all I can truly see—all I can feel—is Kylie being taken without her consent.

It's one thing when the women know—when they're excited—but it's wholly another when they're born into the distinction without a choice or an option to take another road.

"No, she doesn't know," I agree. "She doesn't know her bloodline is special. She doesn't know anything. She's clueless."

Cal drags a hand through his hair. "How the hell is she clueless? I've heard of women not wanting to be a part of it, but they always *know*—"

"Because someone kept her that way," Kane answers before I can. "Because she wasn't raised in it. Her parents died when she was a baby. I looked it up as soon as Rook started making starry eyes at her."

"Are you fucking sure?" Calloway's gaze stays on me. "Because if we move on this and she knew and wanted it…"

"She doesn't want it," I affirm. *I'm not even sure she'll want me.*

"Some of them think it's a damn status symbol," Kane says through a sigh. "Like being sold to monsters makes them special." He shakes his head. "But that's not Kylie."

I step away from them, pacing once, then again. The garage feels too small. The lights too bright. The walls too close.

"I heard him mention Friday," I say, stopping by the open garage door and looking toward the dark night sky. "At the rink. Private thing. He called it *networking.*"

Kane scoffs. "Networking. Sure."

Calloway's face goes sharper. "He said Friday?"

"Yeah," I confirm. "And he keeps pushing it to her. He won't let go of that date. Of that timeline. He wants her there badly enough, I think they might be eager to get her in hand."

Calloway doesn't hesitate. "They know she's involuntary."

"Yeah," I say. "And she doesn't fucking know about *any* of it. Hell, she's still deciding what she wants for dinner, not whether she wants to disappear to some New York penthouse to be vampire fuel on demand."

Calloway's jaw tightens. "And that makes her—"

"Human," I cut in. "It makes her human."

The words come out sharper than I mean them to, but I can't fight the sting enough to hold them back. None of this is even remotely fair to her because it's not her horse, and it's sure as hell not her rodeo. Our vampire bullshit isn't supposed to be her problem. But it is.

It *very much* is.

"Jesus." Kane scrubs a hand over his face. "Not going to lie, this is all pretty fucked. I mean, *fuck.* This is *fucked.*"

"So, Friday," Cal says, his voice hesitant. "You think that's when they move."

Unfortunately, I know it is. I can feel it in flesh and bone.

"And you think you can stop it," Kane chimes in.

"I don't think anything, Kane. I know. Both what I *have* to do and what that means for me—and you guys, as it were." My laugh is soft and sardonic. "Sorry about that."

"Rook…" Calloway's voice softens, just a fraction. "Are you sure about this? Maybe there's…another way."

I almost laugh. If there were another way, I would have taken it. I didn't want this. I didn't fucking want this at all.

What I want is to go back to before I really saw her. I want to go back to before my body recognized her like a command and my instincts turned into a leash. What I want is for her to stay human and safe and unaware.

What I want is to hate her.

But I don't. *Not even close.*

I stare out into the night, and my brothers don't push anymore. They know my silence is my answer.

"She thinks I hate her," I say finally.

"What?" Cal asks.

"She asked me last night when I was fixing her tire," I grind out, jaw tight. "Why I hate her."

Calloway's expression shifts, and understanding flickers in his eyes. Kane lets out a rough laugh.

Their bad news just got worse—we're starting this whole death-sentence adventure off at square fucking zero.

"I told her I hate everyone," I continue flatly. Because I do. Especially any motherfucker who wants to be around her, put their hands on her, *touch* her.

Kane grins. "Wow. You're such a romantic, Rook. Can't wait to convince her we're a safe space, while also fighting for our lives."

Calloway's gaze stays on me. "You didn't tell her anything else?"

"No."

Because if I tell her, she becomes part of it. The moment she knows, she's not just a woman who loves skating and complains about tax season; she's a target who understands she's a target and carries the fear that comes with that.

And the elites don't just take human women with the right bloodlines who are compliant. They revel, too, in the women who resist.

That's a hell of a lot of danger to carry on your own—a burden I won't give *my* fated mate without also providing a cushion for her to land on.

"She doesn't know what waits for her if I don't intervene," I say quietly.

Kane's grin fades. "And you do."

I swallow the lump of rage and guilt that rises in my throat. "Yes."

Calloway's voice drops, careful. "Does she feel it at least? The connection between you?"

I don't answer immediately, even though I'm loaded with the knowledge to do so. She feels it. I know she does. But putting a voice to that makes all of this seem even more real.

It makes a future I never wanted for her inevitable.

"It doesn't matter," I say finally. "Not right now."

Kane steps closer, voice hard. "It matters because, if she's yours—"

"Don't," I snap.

Kane stops. His eyes flare, but he reins it in.

Calloway studies me. "You understand what you're planning."

"Yes."

"You understand that once you intervene, there's no going back."

I understand what it means for me *and* them and that I'm not giving them a say. The answer is still the same.

"Yes."

"And you're prepared to live with what that turns us into."

I hesitate, but it's not because I'm not prepared. It's because I *am*. For whatever may come.

And that means the whole Slater legacy is fucked in one burning basket.

Kane watches me closely. "You're not asking us for permission."

I shake my head, ever so apologetically. "No."

Calloway's mouth tightens. "When?"

"Not yet," I say. "But soon."

Kane laughs once, sharp and humorless. "Bullshit. We're already there."

I don't argue. Because he's right.

I was pulled into that parking lot last night without meaning to be. Called to her house this morning because of Holland's scent. I'm hearing things I shouldn't hear, watching patterns I swore I'd ignore, and making up bullshit excuses about tow trucks and spare tires to put myself between her and Holland, all the while knowing the consequences.

I'm crossing lines I shouldn't be crossing, but I can't find a single cell inside my body that's willing or able to stop.

The next steps will be bolder—but we're already past the point of no return.

"The second he tries to move her," I say, voice steady now, "I'm ending it."

Calloway meets my eyes, his own flaring blue with resignation. "Rook. This doesn't just change things for her," he says. "It changes things for us."

I meet my brother head on. "If you were me, what would you do, Cal?"

His voice is raw. "I'd have already made my move."

9

Y SOME MIRACLE AND ELEMENTARY-AGE DANCE recitals—Martin's youngest daughter's—I'm leaving work by five o'clock on Thursday.

Hallelujah!

When Martin told me he was leaving early, I considered staying anyway so we wouldn't fall behind, but with one look at the dark circles under my eyes, he told me to *spend one godforsaken night being my age for an hour and then go home and get in bed by eight* or he would fire me first thing Friday morning.

I knew the threat was flimsy at best, but far be it for me to look a gift horse in the mouth when everything else in my life has been taking.

My energy, my attention, my guilt.

The universe has been working overtime at draining my cup these days, and without a pitcher and some time, I'll be empty pretty soon.

Once I ensure all the filings I've worked on today have been saved, filed, and backed up three hundred times, I shut down my computer and lock up the office for the night. I waste no time getting to my car—despite nearing April, it's still cold as balls here in Massachusetts, and I forgot my big coat—and drive straight to my favorite coffee shop near the rink.

A fresh cappuccino and a chocolate croissant sound like the perfect treat before I head to the rink and get on the ice for an hour or so.

I'll be skating alone again—Alyssa's already on the road to Connecticut to visit her sick father—and the thought sits heavier than it should. It's not bad. It's just…noticeable.

I tell myself I'm tired and these are just the consequences of a long week, too many late nights, and a brain that won't shut up.

If the next closest rink weren't in downtown Boston, filled with people I don't know *at all*, and an hour commute from my house, I probably would opt for a change of scenery.

But I choose to stick with what I know, even if it doesn't feel quite as relaxing as it used to.

Honey Bee Café isn't usually busy on Thursday evenings—they're more of a morning rush type of place—but tonight, I have to settle for one of the only empty parking spots at the very back of the lot. There's no light overhead, making it extra freaky, so I jump out, slam my door, beep my locks, and move toward the building at a full run, just hoping I don't bust my ass on a patch of black ice.

Thankfully, the smell of coffee, cinnamon, and sugar is quick to make it worth it as the bell above the door announces my entrance. Shelly the owner/operator/decadence extraordinaire's warm welcome doesn't hurt either.

"Well, well, well, if it isn't my favorite customer dragged in from the ether itself."

I laugh. "It's been a rough month, yes, but that kind of flattery will get you everywhere—even if you do say it to everyone who comes through the door."

She grins. "You want your usual, Kylie?"

"You know it."

"Cappuccino and chocolate croissant warmed!" she calls over her shoulder, toward where Deacon and Billy—her only two employees—are busy making drinks.

I pay and wait patiently, and once both my hot cappuccino and plated croissant are in my hands, I head over to a small table by the window to sit down and enjoy my tasties in peace.

I put my phone facedown on the table—the last thing I need is a virtual distraction—and a too-big bite of chocolatey carbs goes straight into my mouth.

It's the perfect mix of ooey, gooey, sweet, and warm, with a hint of salt, and my cheeks bulge comically with the effort to chew the amount I bit off.

It's an annoying little metaphor for life these days and makes me wonder if even entertaining the event with Holland on Friday is smart. I know he's been waxing poetic about the opportunities it could bring via text the past two days, but at this point, it's really feeling like *just one more thing*. Add in the fact that Rook hates—

"Huh," a familiar male voice says from beside me. "I guess it really *is* a small world. First Murray's the other night, and now this…I guess you know all the good places."

I look up to find Holland standing there with a cup in his hand, sleek puffer jacket open, and a friendly smile on his lips. My whole system jolts at the coincidental timing, and a grating tightness fills the space of my chest. I choke down my bite and take a swig of cappuccino to clear it—which tastes just as good—holding up a polite finger until the pathway to answer is free.

"Oh hey, Holland." I try to laugh, but even to my own ears, it sounds a little brittle. He doesn't seem to mind, smiling widely as I remark, "Feeling smaller by the day."

He gestures to the empty chair across from me. "Mind if I sit for a minute?"

"Sure," I reply without a reason to decline other than *that guy Rook who hates you, and I'd rather you didn't.*

Pulling off his jacket and draping it over the back of the chair like he's preparing to stay awhile, he settles in and wraps both his hands around his own cup.

"I hope you won't take this the wrong way, Ky, but you look tired. Is it work? Something else? I can be a listening ear if you'd like."

I snort, both at him and to myself, because I must have reached a new point for myself if the guy I thought was chasing me around to try to get in my pants is actually just *concerned* for me.

My God, Kylie. If this isn't a wake-up call that I'm pushing myself to burnout, I don't know what is.

"Hah, yeah. No offense taken," I say. "I work for an accountant, and this tax season has been…chaos. I'm not surprised I look like the walking dead."

He winces. "I don't envy you."

"What about you?" I ask. "You always look like you're coming from somewhere important. Is your job serious? Stressful?"

He smiles at that, like it's a private joke. If I had to guess, he likes the idea that I think he does something important, but to be honest, I'm genuinely too tired for a full psychoanalysis. "Law firm. Boston."

"Really?"

"Yeah. Big one," he says easily. "Mostly contracts. Talent-adjacent stuff. It can definitely get stressful, but it's mostly…" He shrugs, a smile creasing the corners of his caramel eyes so much, it's almost as though they darken. "Fun."

I tilt my head. "Talent-adjacent? That sounds like an NDA or two are involved."

"Agents. Investors. People in the entertainment industry," he explains with a laugh. "It's not as glamorous as you'd think, but it's interesting. And, yes. Privacy is at the utmost premium."

"No offense, but that seems like a pretty heady job for someone who doesn't look a day over twenty-five."

He puts a hand to his chest, mock flattered. "Twenty-nine, technically, which I suppose is still a little young." He shrugs and smiles. "But I skipped a few grades in elementary and ended up starting college at sixteen. I guess that puts me a bit ahead of the curve."

"Wow. That's impressive," I say, because it *is* impressive. I barely tolerated college at eighteen, nineteen, and twenty, let alone sixteen. If it weren't for Gammy, I probably would have dropped out. Not because I wasn't smart enough, but because it was just so…ordinary. Which I know is rich coming from someone working in an accountancy firm and dreaming of an early bedtime now, but when I was younger, I always thought my life would be bigger or more interesting or…something.

Talent-adjacent, perhaps.

He waves it off. "Anyway. Where has the other girl you usually skate with been? Alyssa, right?"

"Yeah, Alyssa," I say. "She's my roommate. Normally, she'd be here now, but she's out of town this weekend."

"Oh?" His tone is light but inquisitive. "Everything okay?"

"Sort of. She went to Connecticut for the weekend. Her dad's been sick for a while," I explain. "It's been hard for her…balancing school and going home to be with family."

"That's rough," he says.

"Yeah," I agree. Putting myself in Alyssa's shoes somehow always places my current woes in perspective. I know what it's like to lose your parents, but at least it happened to me before they were such a big part of my life. At this point, a world with her dad in it is all she knows.

"And what about you? You staying put this weekend?"

"Mostly," I reply. "Trying to recover. I'll probably spend time with my grandmother Saturday, though."

"Lucky," he says. "I don't have any family close…well, other than the guys on my team." He shakes his head. "They're probably not too happy with me tonight, though, because I missed a game. Work ran late."

He glances toward the window, where the rink sign is visible down the street. Compulsorily, I follow his line of sight with my own, visions of Rook Slater dancing in both my eyes and another, deeper place I'd rather not discuss.

I don't know how my body can be so freaking interested in a man who doesn't even know how to smile.

"Who'd you play?"

"Iron Knights." It's the team I was hoping to hear and,

begrudgingly, makes my heart skip a tiny beat. *If I get to the rink soon, Rook might still be there.*

"Ah, yes. The most heated rivalry in Concordia Rec League," I joke. "Bet you're missing the chance to shed some of their blood."

He laughs, and I push my luck.

"What is it between you guys, by the way? Is it just the hockey? Something else? I always feel like games between your two teams take ugliness to a new level."

Holland's eyes shutter briefly before he brushes me off diplomatically. "Oh, you know how it is sometimes. Grew up together. Never got along. We just don't see eye to eye on a lot of stuff, and most of my guys and I are over the immaturity, you know?"

I hum my acquiescence, but the truth is, I *don't* know. That nonanswer gave me exactly zero point two five out of a million when it comes to real reasoning.

"Well, I better head over now anyway," I say, swigging my still-too-full cappuccino and shrugging. "I'm planning on skating after it's done, and I don't want to have a late night."

"Figures," he says with a grin. "That is your usual routine."

A piercingly sharp pain zaps my head at Holland's mention of my *usual routine*, but it's gone as quick as it came. I don't know if it's a stress headache trying to form or an aneurysm or something else, but I chalk it up to one weird moment and move on.

He grins, seemingly unaware of my phantom pain and drifting mind. "So…about Friday…still no pressure, but maybe if I give a clearer picture of what it actually is, you'll feel better about it."

"Okay," I agree, knowing the fastest route sometimes is directly through the forest. For whatever reason, Holland Thorne is fixated on me and this thing Friday, and if I don't let him finish now, he'll chase me around until he can.

"It's very low-key. Private event that includes people from my firm and a few folks from New York, and I know that can sound intimidating, but I think you'd actually like it. Free drinks and dancing and food and maybe some connections that could give you a once-in-a-lifetime opportunity to do something big."

"It all sounds really interesting, but I'm not sure an event of that scale is a great way to make my best impression. I tend to… lock up…in large crowds."

"I get that. I do," he replies immediately, offering a soft smile. "But just remember that I'd be there with you, okay? And if you get there and can only stay for five minutes, we'd leave. No questions asked."

I shrug. "I'll think about it, okay? But I'm leaning toward yes." It's as big a commitment as the one I gave my grandmother for pot roast night—aka under duress and mostly against my will—and everything in my head is already yelling at me to cancel. But I guess I'm hoping if I seem more committed, he'll drop it for a while.

He smiles hugely before checking his watch and jumping up from the table.

"Oh shit. I didn't realize it was so late. I better get over to the rink." He winks at me. "See how many teeth we lost tonight."

Effectively, it seems, my theory worked. At least temporarily.

"Good idea." I laugh. "I'll probably see you over there."

"I certainly hope so." He smiles and waves as he heads through the door, tossing his full cup of coffee into the trash at its side.

I sit there for a second longer than I mean to as the oddest, most unsettled feeling takes up shop in my gut. Nothing about our conversation was rude or inappropriate or even uncomfortable, really. He was nice and listened intently when I was talking and met my eyes with no trouble at all.

But something about it feels…I don't know…off.

And when I stand to gather my things, the feeling doesn't leave with him.

I push it aside, offer a wave to Shelly, Deacon, and Billy behind the counter, and head out of Honey Bee Café to make the two-minute journey to Concordia Rec Rink.

Rook's Suburban is obvious when I enter the parking lot, and despite myself, a small thrill takes flight in my stomach.

I grab my bag and hustle inside, jolting slightly at the boisterous, violent sounds of a hockey game the instant I step through the door.

The rivalry game, it seems, is still fully in progress.

It takes me an embarrassingly short amount of time to locate Rook on the bench. His helmet is off, the sweat from his effort in the game darkening his already dark hair to onyx, and his body is coiled tight, even at rest.

He's looking at me.

Not casually and not like he's surprised to see me. His gaze is…fixed. Like he's been waiting for something and doesn't know whether it's arrived or not.

His brother Kane sits next to him, laughing with one of their teammates in his usual jovial way, while Calloway continues their penchant for damage on the ice, but it's Rook's tension-filled gaze that makes me feel the quietest.

There's something sharp in his expression. Anger, maybe.

Tension. Whatever it is, it makes my stomach tighten instead of bristle.

His focus shifts suddenly, and I realize Holland has stepped up behind me.

"Glad I got to have coffee with you tonight, Kylie," Holland says quietly. "Have a good skate."

"Thanks," I reply, turning back toward the rink.

Rook's eyes are no longer on me. They're dark and unblinking and locked on Holland's retreating back.

And when I glance out onto the ice, Calloway has stopped skating entirely. He's staring straight at me from center ice, his expression mirroring Rook's in a way that makes no sense at all.

My brows draw together.

Okay.

What the actual hell is going on?

10

ROOK

I SHOULD'VE PLAYED BETTER TONIGHT—I WAS half a second slow at least a dozen times and completely off focus the majority of the game—but even among the noise of the locker room crashing around me as my teammates lament our loss, I can't find a fuck inside myself to give.

My head wasn't on the ice during the game.

My head was on Honey Bee Café.

On Holland Slimefuck Thorne.

On Kylie Moon.

I don't give a shit about hockey or championships or rec-league reputations. I care that something has shifted, and I don't like the direction it's moving.

Monsters don't circle forever. They wait until they're sure.

None of this shit is fair for her—and yet, I fear to the absolute root of my existence that fair's long gone and danger is well-seated in its place anyway.

I yank the second skate loose and look up to find Cal chest-to-chest with evil himself at the door. I know he heard Holland's remark about enjoying coffee with Kylie, and this is his way of doing damage control.

Because where he's steady, I'm an earthquake—I will rock Holland's shit into the next fucking solar system at the first smart comment, if given the opportunity.

Kane moves to Cal's back as Holland's guys, Mark and Evan, step up behind him out of the shadows, and I jump from my spot on the bench and head their direction too.

They don't have gear bags because they didn't play tonight, too busy following her to grace us with their normal fake injuries and whiny little bitchiness.

Holland catches my eye, essentially ignoring Cal and Kane, and smiles. "Didn't make the game," he says casually. "Busy night."

He's trying to bait me into losing my cool or giving away something about how much I know so he has insight into how locked in I am on her, but thankfully, I'm too invested to take it.

I know his tactics. I know his moves. And I know that if he can rile me with a simple remark, Kylie's already in way more danger than she should be.

"It's a shame, though," he continues. "I was really looking forward to kicking some Slater ass."

Even the curse seems foreign on his silver tongue. I roll my eyes. They might think they're all fucking mighty, but they're just a bunch of pussies.

Slow and deliberate, I move closer, easing Cal out of the way so I can give Holland my full attention. "You know the rules. If you didn't play tonight, you shouldn't be back here."

One of his guys shifts, but Holland just holds up a hand. A silent gesture not to react. Quite a fucking pity, to be honest. I have so much anger and so much rage vibrating through my goddamn bones, it'd be cathartic for one of his goons to test me.

"Relax, *Garbage Man*," he says, practically spitting. "We were just heading out."

Garbage Man. I shake my head and smile. He *really* wants me to lose my cool, but I already know these games—how the elites and their gofers load and aim the gun while taping your fucking hand to it and then blame you for pulling the trigger.

And I refuse to leave her to fend for herself against these fucking bloodsucking, power-hungry vultures.

When Holland and his goons don't move, I point toward the exit.

"The door is that way."

"Wow, Rook." Kane lets out a quiet laugh. "They really do need everything spelled out for them."

Holland's jaw tightens. "The way I heard it, you're the ones who sucked at hockey tonight."

Cal stares at him. "Pretty sure no one is talking about hockey right now."

Holland's smile thins. "The Slaters are a little touchy this evening, huh?"

I don't respond to that, but I don't have to. It's a question as obvious as the elephant in the room, and Holland does everything short of acknowledging it completely when he glances toward the door—toward the hallway that leads back to the rink.

Toward *Kylie.*

"Maybe I'll hang around for a while." He smiles, observing me closely. "There's just something about watching her skate, you know…"

My fists clench and my jaw ticks under the strain of my in-stinctual drive to kill him, and because I can't without leaving Kylie even more vulnerable than she already is, he gets a hash mark in his win column.

He laughs with too much ego and not enough sense. It's the hearty ha-ha-ha you can only let loose when you think you're invincible.

It will come back to bite him, though. I'm surer of what I have to do than ever.

"You're entirely predictable, Garbage Man," Holland says lightly. "I'm not sorry to say, that'll be your downfall."

This asshole. He's so fucking cocky, but I'd rather be a garbage man than a gofer for the elites. I'd rather be *dead* than be him.

And soon, he'll realize just how willing I am to prove it.

"How about you worry about your own shit, goferboy," I reply.

"Oh, but I am." His gaze flicks back to mine. "That's kind of the problem." He steps closer to me. It's not enough to provoke, but it's just enough to encroach on my space.

Kane and Cal both crowd my back, ready to set a whole fuck-ing explosion in motion if they have to. Evan and Mark do the same behind Holland.

"I know what you're doing. I know what you're trying to do. And you know better than this, *Rook,*" he says quietly. "Don't get attached to her."

I don't move, but my jaw is pure steel. "Say her name."

He doesn't. That's deliberate too.

"That blood…" Holland continues, voice low, smooth. "It's not for you, and you know it. Step aside."

"Over my dead body," I declare.

Holland's smile is foretelling. "That can be arranged."

"You have no ownership rights, and you know it. To any of them. And the time for you and your masters to do whatever the fuck you want is running out."

Holland chuckles. "Clearly, I need to remind you how things work." He steps even closer to me. "Walk away from her, or pay the price."

Walking away isn't an option. *She is mine.*

"You know, Holland, things work until they don't work anymore. Something tells me we're right on the cusp of you finding that out."

His eyes flash. "Careful, Slater."

"Careful what?"

He shakes his head, smiling again and disengaging by taking a step back. "It doesn't matter. After tomorrow, she won't be your concern."

That isn't a threat; it's a *promise.*

He straightens and claps his hands once. "Come on, boys. Let's get out of here before we start smelling like fucking *trash.*"

Cal waits a beat before following them out of the locker room and into the parking lot to *listen*, and Kane stays back to calm me.

"You all right?" he asks, trying to push me back to the bench to sit down, but I muscle past him instead.

"Rook. Hey. Rook, where are you going?"

I'm shirtless, still in half of my gear and my feet only covered by a pair of fucking socks, but I don't give a shit. There's only one place I need to be, and I need to be there yesterday.

Kylie's by the bleachers, bag at her feet, and pulling her hair back like she's about to take the ice when I get to her. She looks normal and calm and completely fucking unaware, and because I don't have time to be careful, I nearly startle her right off the bench and onto the floor with how fast I approach her.

"Kylie, you need to go home," I say immediately, my tone heavy with demand.

"Oh hey, Rook." She snorts, gathering herself. "Hello to you too."

"You need to go home," I state again, too worked up to soften that shit at all.

Her eyes narrow in offense. "Excuse me?"

I can't fucking blame her, but this isn't a time for naïveté-necessitating lengthy explanations. Holland admitted it himself—she's not safe at all, and after tomorrow, I won't be able to save her. "You need to go home. Now."

"What?" Confusion replaces affront as she takes in my clearly agitated expression. "Why?"

I open my mouth, but then I quickly close it. There's no going back once I open the Pandora's box of information.

The existence of vampires, her destiny to be with one, her blood's value—and the corrupt nature of the wealthy that transcends her species—aren't the kinds of things that put a woman's already anxious mind at ease.

They're the kinds of things that send even the strongest into a spiral.

"You shouldn't be here, Kylie," I say as gently as I can manage.

"What do you mean, I shouldn't be here?" Her expression hardens. "I have every right to be here, Rook. The game is over. The ice is free."

"This isn't about the ice being free, Ky. This is about listening to me because I'm asking you to," I say with a groan she wrongly interprets as frustration with her.

"Pretty sure I'm under no obligation to do anything under command, from you or otherwise, without an explanation. The only one who makes decisions for Kylie Kay Moon is *me*."

"I'm not trying to rule your life, I swear." I sigh. "I know I'm not the man who paints the room with flowery faces and smooth lines and even a fucking smile. I know. But I'm asking you, please, to leave this rink right now and go straight home."

She stares at me like she doesn't recognize the man in front of her, both because of my demands and the temporary bout of kindness. I can see it scares her—her pulse is thrumming like a hummingbird's wings—but there's at least a tiny break in the wall between us too.

She can *feel* it. This *thing*, my intentions, my desperation.

She lets out a deep sigh. "I came here to skate. Like I always do, Rook. I don't see what the big deal is or why I can't have this *tiny*, stupid moment for myself."

She squints now, on the verge of tears as she fights against the war I've started inside her. I get it. I get it so much, and yet, I still have to be the asshole. Because people are watching us now—people, including Holland, who's evidently returned to the ring for a second round.

Our enemies are too close for comfort and, at this point, may be making moves to preempt me by striking tonight, rather than tomorrow.

I lower my voice. "Please just go home."

Her eyes narrow. "No."

"*Yes.*"

"No."

Fuck. "Jesus, Ky. Now is *not* the time to be a stubborn pain in my ass."

Her jaw drops. "What did you just call me?"

Goddammit. Fuck this whole fucked-up situation.

I close my eyes, pleading with myself for patience. "Kylie. I'm begging you. On my metaphorical, grumpy knees, to please, please, go home."

"You know what?" She huffs, abruptly tugging at the laces of her skates. "Fine. I'm going home. I'm going home and nailing the damn doors shut like a coffin until I escape whatever nightmare's asshole this week climbed from."

"Kylie, I—"

"Shut up. Just shut the hell up." She rips her skates off her feet and tosses them into her bag. Her hoodie is pulled over her head next, and her bag is on her shoulder within seconds.

"I don't know what your issue is," she adds, eyes blazing, "but tonight is the last time I let you make it my problem. How about, in the future, just leave me the hell alone, okay?"

She storms past me, but mad is better than dead.

She disappears down the hallway and out into the parking lot.

I hear her car start and the tires roll away from the rink.

And I just stand there, staring at the empty space she left behind. I know that Holland and his cronies are still here. I know I'm on the precipice of an absolute shitstorm for myself and my brothers.

I know all the fucking things.

But she left because I asked her to, and that tells me she has the kind of fight in her that could keep her alive.

It's a small mercy, but a mercy, nonetheless.

There's no going back now, and I know tomorrow won't be like this.

Tomorrow, they won't ask. They'll just *take*.

And I already know what I'm going to have to do before that happens.

11

KYLIE

I'M STILL STEWING TWO HOURS AFTER LEAVING the rink, and God help me, doing exactly as Rook ordered by coming straight home. There's no food in the fridge, there's nothing on the TV, and for a Thursday that seemed born of miracles, it's sure left me foul and fighting in a canoe up shit's creek now.

"I'm telling you, Alyssa, this guy is ballsy. At first, I thought it was nice that he was always coming to my rescue and inserting himself into my chaos at his own expense, but at this point, it's like he has some sort of ownership over me. Like he has the power to make my decisions and control my life. I'm fucking done. Done with it, you hear me?" I rant, slamming down onto the sofa and ramming my hand into the bucket of cheeseballs she left behind.

She laughs, the muffled static of her parents' Connecticut house phone making her sound more nasal than normal, and I cram my mouth full of balls.

"Oh yeah, I can hear you, babe. Your volume is at an eleven on a scale of one to five. And I get it. I do. You're an independent gal with a lifetime of experience in taking care of yourself because you had to. Some grumpy asshole giving you orders? It's ridiculous."

"Yes," I agree, "it is."

She snorts before continuing. "But, if I may, without you biting my head off…can I make a hypothesis of my own?"

"I guess," I snap so harshly it comes out like a bark, and she laughs again.

"Right. Well…what if I told you I don't think Rook Slater thinks he owns you? That I don't think he's trying to control your life or insert himself into your decisions or cross the line. But instead…what if I were to suggest that, maybe, just maybe…he *likes* you. And all this inserting himself is because he's *jealous*."

"I think you live in a fantasy world of rom-coms and toxic masculinity, Lyss. Sometimes red flags are just red fucking flags."

"Yes. That's true. I know better than anyone because I've had my taste of a fair share of assholes. "But Rook is…grumpy, sure. Closed off. But he's never struck me as dangerous. Not until Holland started sniffing and pissing around you like a rabid dog, that is."

"You know what, Alyssa? Even if that is the case…fuck that. I don't need some guy going psycho every time one of his rivals dares to look at me. I need a Prince-Charming-type, you know? Romance and flowers and wooing and shit." I groan before shoving the bucket of balls to the side and letting them slide off onto the floor.

It's the first good luck of the night that they land right side up.

"I don't know," I whine. "Maybe I'll just take off right now and drive to Gammy's house tonight. Call Martin and tell him I've come down with the sick-of-men's-shit virus and lick my wounds in an environment that comes with home-cooked meals."

"That's not an entirely bad idea."

"Yeah. I'm doing it—"

"*But,*" she cuts me off, her tone both deliberate and loud enough to pause my roll off the couch. "Not tonight. Call Martin in the morning, take your time getting ready without the rush of making it to the office, stop for breakfast at that place on Bleaker Street that you love—"

"Bacon, Egg, and Freeze?" I say wistfully, dreaming of the everything bagel, Benedict-style hollandaise, and perfectly crispy bacon I haven't made time for in two whole months.

"Uh-huh," she agrees. "And just…let yourself be quiet for once. Take a nice bath tonight, put on some relaxing music, and set your phone to silent. You've been in overload for too long, and your nervous system is totally and completely fucked."

"Great. I love the sound of that."

She snorts. "It's not permanent, Ky. Have a quiet night and go to your grandma's tomorrow. Leave all the Rook and Holland bullshit for them to figure out by taking yourself out of the equation for a little while. See how you feel next week, after all the dust settles, and if it's still annoying, fuck both those guys right out of your life."

I cackle. "Fuck them off, or fuck them, fuck them like you would fuck them?"

"Both. Neither. None. Whatever you like."

I sigh. "Okay. I like this suggestion. I do feel a little bad because Holland has been practically begging me all week to come to his work event tomorrow night, but…I just can't. I need a step back."

She giggles. "Girlfriend, with a name like Holland, he's practically begging you to run away."

"I always found it kind of interesting," I defend, and she guffaws, full-on gal-pal gossip engaged.

"Oh, please. *You* would think a name like that is interesting."

"You bitch."

I can hear her smile through the phone. "That's right, baby. And proud of it. Every sweet gal like you needs a sidekick like me, and you know it."

I nod, admitting, "I would be lost without you, I'm afraid." Licking my lips, I force myself to ask the thing neither one of us wants me to ask, and yet the thing I know she needs me to the most. "How's your dad?"

"Not his best. But hanging in there. We all are."

"Lyss, if there's anything I can do, you know—"

"Yeah, yeah, can it, you overworking troll. Worry about yourself for once, okay?"

"I'll try."

"Good. Call me tomorrow if you want, when you get to Gammy's. You can let me live vicariously through her cooking on the phone."

"Your mom still struggling, huh?"

She chortles. "To put it mildly. My dad has always been the one with the kitchen chops."

Instead of lingering on the sad note, I move on. I know she wants me to.

"Okay, you got it. I'll call you when I'm safely to Gammy's

and regale you with tales of leftover pot roast, buttered biscuits, and chicken potpie."

"Can't wait." I smile, but her voice drops just the tiniest of notes before continuing. "And, Ky?"

"Yeah?"

"Be careful, okay? Just in case Rook is right."

"I will. Promise."

We hang up, and I switch my ringer to silent, toss my phone to the coffee table, and lean back on the couch.

I only mean to take a little rest before my bubble bath, but before I know it, I'm fast asleep.

12

ROOK

As Friday morning comes, I'm up with the rise of the sun.

While vampires don't need sleep to survive, living among humans for so long has forced me into the habit of pretending. I lie down at night like everyone else and close my eyes until daylight turns the back of my eyelids orange.

But last night was different. Worry plagued me, and a knot in my stomach got tighter and tighter by the hour. Kane and Calloway showed up around midnight and practically sat vigil over me, and now, while they shower in my bathroom and the guest bath of my two-bedroom, respectively, I find myself staring into the soft glow of the sky.

I stand on the porch, arms braced on the railing, jaw locked hard enough to hurt.

The more I stare, the angrier I get.

All fucking males. That's what vampires have been for generations now, and no one should dare question it.

But fuck, I am motherfucking questioning it.

There are no daughters or sisters. No balance at all. Just

vampire sons born into bloodlines and archaic hierarchies that were decided long before birth.

You're either an elite or you're a nobody—like me.

Female vampires are so rare they may as well be the unicorns of the vampire world. In all my years of life, I've never met one, never seen one, and never known one to be born or alive. They require elite vampire blood and the right human bloodlines and fated mates. All three of those things have to align in order for a female vampire to be born into this mortal world.

But the elites have made damn sure that alignment stopped happening.

As long as they control the bloodlines—auctioning women, hoarding the rare ones, blocking fated bonds before they ever take root—no new female vampires are born. Just more males. More soldiers. More pieces on their board. More worker bees to control.

Vampires outside the elite bloodline? We can only produce sons. A design flaw—or maybe a design feature—depending on who's benefiting.

And the vamps who were turned from humans? The old, reckless ones from centuries back? They can't reproduce at all. But that's not technically a bad thing. Turning humans has never been a good idea. All it does is create unstable, blood-hungry monsters who need blood to survive instead of choosing it. It's basically been outlawed for generations now.

So here we are. A world full of male vampires. A shrinking number of human women with the blood that matters. And elites who've figured out how to choke the system just enough to keep their power intact.

If it weren't all so damn stereotypical, maybe it wouldn't be so bad, but unfortunately, it's exactly as you'd expect. The rich get richer, and do whatever the fuck they want, while those of us at the bottom of the pyramid have to play the hand we're dealt.

The middle of the pile, though—that's the real problem.

I hate the elites, but I *really* hate their fucking gofers, the fucks in the middle class. They're tail-grabbers, hanger-on-ers, and wannabes with no sense of their pathetic nature.

They think they're something, their egos inflating to the stratosphere like Holland's clearly has, but they're really just a tool. They're in charge of the dirty work, the bidding, and the day-to-day snobbery, while the elites keep to their penthouses and fancy mansions. They're clean—without even having to wash their hands.

And now, it's not just theoretical. It's not tangential.

It's *mine*. My problem, my mate, my fucking law to break.

Cal steps onto the porch beside me, his tanned hand running through still-wet hair as he pulls a T-shirt over his head.

I don't balk or turn or move as I whisper, "I've got a really bad feeling. I think it's happening before we thought."

Cal snorts. "All of your feelings are bad, bro. All of them. Since the moment we've been old enough to talk and walk and cogitate, I've not gotten one good feeling off you, period."

He's not entirely wrong—I *am* a grumpy asshole with a whole cesspool of bad feelings and angry outbursts—but it's not easy being the one with the weight of the whole Slater world on my shoulders.

We grew up orphaned, and as the oldest, I fell naturally into the role of duty and worry. As vampires without parents, we were forced to grow up in a world we didn't understand, with people who didn't understand us, all the while trying to figure out how the hell to keep pretty much every facet of our differentness a secret.

I carried the weight of both myself and my younger brothers on my shoulders. Ironically, this is the first selfish thing I've done in our whole lives—and it might just be fucked enough to end them.

"This is different, Cal."

"A connection thing?"

I shrug. "I guess. I feel like I'm being eaten alive from the inside out."

And then, I say the one and only thing that's circling my mind. "They're not waiting, Cal. They're moving in."

That's the thing about gofers like Holland—they don't circle unless the outcome is already decided.

Cal leans forward, forearms on the railing. "You want to tell me what you're thinking?"

I close my eyes.

Because if I say it out loud, it becomes real.

"They won't ask," I say finally. "Not today."

Cal doesn't argue. He's tall enough to reach the soffit, and he puts his hands to it to lean forward. "So…what do we need to do?"

The answer sits heavy in my mouth.

"You're not going to like it."

He chuckles, his big white teeth shining in a sardonic smile. "Yeah, well, what else is new? There hasn't been a single thing about this phase of life I've liked yet. And, I imagine, there won't be for a long time. Doesn't mean it's not the right thing to do."

I nod. "Yeah. I guess you're correct."

"Okay, so…what? What's the plan?"

I turn to face him. "We go for a drive."

"A drive to where, Rook?"

"Kylie's house."

Cal goes still. "You mean—"

"Yes," I cut him off before he can question. Before he can waste any more time with nuances. "I take her before they can."

"Fuck, Rook." He swears under his breath, but then he laughs. "Well, *fuck.*"

"I know."

"That's certainly crossing a line we've never crossed. A line we won't be able to uncross."

"I know."

He searches my face. He knows I'm not wrong. But he also knows that if I don't do anything, if I don't make a move, she disappears.

Cal exhales, long and slow.

"Cal, I'm asking you to help me make sure she's still alive tomorrow."

He nods once before letting out a harsh laugh and turning back toward the house. "Kane!"

A door opens. Footsteps. Kane appears in the doorway with a towel around his neck.

"What's up?"

"Get the Suburban ready," Cal says.

Kane's gaze flicks to me, and I swear it looks like he's fighting a smile. "Where are we going, bro?"

I swallow. "Kylie's."

"And when we get there?"

I don't dress it up. "I don't give her a choice."

The words taste like blood, but the smile Kane was fighting is now front and center on his face.

"Let's do it!"

No hesitancy. No questioning. Just full acceptance that what we're about to do will change everything.

I'll be a kidnapper.

It sounds preposterous, but in less than an hour, it'll be reality.

And there's no going back from that.

13

KYLIE

A LOUD BANG JERKS ME AWAKE. I SIT UP straight on the couch and fight to find my bearings. The sun is already up, shining through the light fog in the living room side window, and the red numbers on the microwave blare a new day in the kitchen.

I'm confused and weary, but when another bang sounds from outside on the street, I move on sheer instinct alone.

Shit! The freaking garbage! I must've forgotten again!

Bolting off the couch, I race toward the garage door on shaky legs and adrenaline. Unlocking it brusquely, I lean out and hit the clicker for the overhead door and take the steps down to the concrete three at a time.

Cold air hits my face as the garage door rises, and I time my exit, skittering under the door with just enough clearance to hit the driveway at a run.

But my feet skid to a stop when I come face-to-face with two men in dark suits walking toward me. There's no garbage truck. No Rook. Just a blacked-out Escalade sitting in my driveway, idling in place.

That's when it hits me—it's not Tuesday. It's Friday.

And I don't know these men at all.

"Kylie Moon?" the taller of the two calls out. His voice is calm and neutral, like he's a teacher taking attendance.

Every hair on my body stands up.

The men close the distance between us quickly, though they're still standing a good twenty feet from me when they come to a stop.

They look too put together for this to be random, but they don't look official in any sense of the word I've ever known. They're not in police uniforms. They don't have badges. If anything, they're dressed in fancy suits I'm more likely to see in an advertisement for Dior than at the department store at the Concordia Mall.

"W-who are you?" My voice is thin, and my hands shake as an overwhelming sense of fear consumes my nerves.

"We're here to bring you somewhere safe," the tall man says, his voice still eerily calm. "There's been a concern."

"A concern?" My stomach falls to my feet. "What? Who are you? What are you talking about?"

The other man, the shorter of the two, with eyes so light they seem almost translucent in the sun, takes steps closer to me. "Just come with us, and we'll get everything straightened out."

His palms are out and his shoulders are relaxed. His posture isn't threatening, but he removes ten feet of distance between us with his strides. "I can assure you, it's for your safety."

When I don't respond or make any moves to walk toward them, he frowns.

"There's no need to make this difficult. Just come with us."

"I don't know who you are." My throat tightens. "I—I'm not going anywhere with you."

The taller man gives a small sigh like I'm inconveniencing him.

"I understand you're confused," he says. "But you need to come with us now. It's very important."

"No." My head is already shaking back and forth, like my body is responding before my brain can. "I think you need to get off my property." I take a step back toward my garage. The concrete is ice-cold under my bare feet, but my brain barely registers it.

A third man appears from the passenger side of the Escalade. He's taller and broader than the two guys standing in front of me and moving with determined steps. "There's no need to worry. We're going to keep you safe."

His words should be reassuring, but they only make my pulse hit Olympian-sprinter-level speeds.

"You need to leave."

"Listen," the man with the light eyes says. "We can do this the easy way, or we can do this the hard way."

My mouth goes dry. "I'm calling the police."

He doesn't react to that threat—none of them does—and that's the most terrifying part.

Every instinct in my body tells me to *run*.

I fumble to get back into the garage, feet slipping as I try to move as quick as I can, but before I can get beneath the door, a hand clamps over my wrist and yanks me back a few feet.

I freeze, and when I look up, I find the tallest man of the three invading my personal space. His eyes are narrowed and dark in ways my brain can't comprehend.

When I try to yank my hand away from his hold, he leans toward me so we're almost nose to nose. "Don't," he says, his voice harsh.

I want to scream, but when I open my mouth, nothing comes out. My breath is sharp and frantic, and I twist my arm back and forth manically, trying to pull free from him.

But his grip just tightens around my wrist.

"Stop, Kylie. We don't have time for this."

How he even knows my name when I've never seen him in my entire life makes my panic spike into something that feels a lot like lava. "Let go of me!"

I try to scream again, but it comes out strangled.

"Relax—" he starts to say, already dragging me toward their Escalade, but another voice cuts through the air.

"Take your hand off her."

The man stops, and I turn my head to find Rook Slater walking up my driveway. He's not in his uniform or work boots, but in jeans and a dark jacket, hair messy like he didn't sleep. His eyes are locked on the man still gripping my wrist, and this isn't the grumpy demeanor I've grown accustomed to.

It's harsher. Sharper. And it looks like he would burn the world down *for* me rather than against me.

Kane and Calloway follow behind him.

Kane is looking directly at Rook, while Calloway's gaze slides over the men like he's counting them.

"Rook Slater." The man with the light eyes smiles faintly. "We heard some rumblings. Guess I shouldn't be surprised to see you here."

Rook doesn't smile back.

"This doesn't involve you," the man still holding my wrist says.

"Yeah, it does." Rook takes one more step forward. "Because it involves her."

"She's coming with us," the man says.

Rook tilts his head slightly. "No."

And then, he moves.

It's not fast like a normal person fast, but fast like my brain can't keep up with what I'm seeing. One second, he's standing there. The next, the man holding my wrist is within Rook's grasp, and choking sounds are coming from his lungs.

I stumble back, wrist suddenly free, but shock making my knees weak. It takes all my strength to stay on my feet.

The man with the light eyes lunges and Kane intercepts him like a truck hitting a deer, and the impact is loud and violent in ways that make their hockey brawls look like child's play.

Calloway's already on the other man, shoving him back against the Escalade with a sound that makes me flinch.

Someone swears. Someone grunts. Something cracks.

Everything is happening faster than my eyes can track, but the man who grabbed my arm is on the ground now and his eyes look lifeless.

Oh my God! Is he dead?!

My heart hammers so hard in my chest that it hurts.

But it feels like someone puts life in slow motion when Rook turns toward me. His eyes find mine, and the urgency and command in his voice are undeniable.

"Kylie," he says. "We have to go."

"Who? What is—?"

"Now, Kylie!" he shouts, and his tone slices through me. "We have to go now."

But I'm frozen in place. My head bobs back and forth, my mind a disoriented swirl of fragmented thoughts. "Rook, I—"

"I'm sorry, Ky," Rook says in apology as he gets even closer, my feet now treading backward toward the garage. "Really, I am."

"Rook…" I beg, both knowing what's coming and praying I'm wrong. "Please. Don't."

He's on me in less than a second, pinning my arms to my sides and hoisting me over his shoulder like I weigh nothing. I open my mouth to scream and do it loudly. "Rook, no! Put me down!" I gasp, kicking instinctively.

He doesn't.

He carries me across the driveway and toward their Suburban idling at the curb. Kane is already at the driver's side, yanking the back door open.

"Rook!" I fight harder, pure terror taking over. "What are you doing?"

His jaw is locked so tight it trembles. "Saving your life."

"By kidnapping me?!"

"You can hate me later," he snaps. "Right now, you're breathing."

I open my mouth to scream at the top of my lungs, but Cal is there already, holding a hand over my mouth while Kane keeps hold of my legs.

I scratch and fight as hard as I can to no avail as the three brothers carry me to their Suburban. I swear, even if I'd have been able to get a scream out through Cal's hand, it wouldn't have been loud enough to wake anyone.

Rook shoves me into the back seat. It's neither gentle nor cruel, but efficient.

Calloway hops into the front passenger seat, slamming the door, and Kane peels out so fast my head snaps back against the seat.

The locks click automatically.

The world outside blurs.

I twist, trying to look back through the rear window.

The black SUV. My house. The men.

Did they kill all of them?!

But it's gone behind a curve of forest and houses before I can make sense of what just happened. Before I can even know if those men are alive or if they're dead or if they're currently in the Escalade following us.

Terror grips me, as the very worst-case scenario in every woman's mind grabs me by the tits and drags me to the deep end of its waters.

There were three men I didn't know trying to force me to go with them to an undisclosed location for completely undisclosed reasons, and I'm pretty sure at least one of them is dead in my driveway.

And now, the Slater brothers—whom I do know—have success-fully managed to take me. Against my will.

I'm being kidnapped. Actually fucking taken like some sort of Liam Neeson bullshit without my own Liam to find me. I thought I knew the Slater brothers—Alyssa thought they were harmless.

Turns out we were both really fucking wrong.

Turns out there are a hell of a lot of men in this freaking town we need to be very, very afraid of.

The doors are locked, and the handle doesn't budge as I fight and claw to try to open it. As Kane drives us to an unknown destination, I start begging.

I know this is bad, but maybe, just maybe, I can reason with them before things really get out of hand.

"Guys, guys, please. You don't need to do this. Please just take me to a police station or something. Or better yet, take me to my gammy's. I won't even go to the cops! I won't tell anyone what happened or what you did to those guys, and we can all just go on with our lives, okay?"

"Ky, relax," Rook coaches, his voice as soft as I've ever heard it, which, quite frankly, pisses me right the hell off.

"Relax? *Relax*? I'm pretty sure one of those men back there is dead, and you and your band of brothers just fucking kidnapped me, Rook! If you want me to relax, do relaxing things…how about that?"

"She's funny," Kane remarks from the driver's seat, and without thinking, I throw my arm forward to punch him in the neck.

When he catches my fist with ease—sight unseen—my eyes widen to the edges of my face. Scooting back gently, I press myself into the leather of the seat and gulp.

"What the hell is going on here? Who were those men? And why, why, *why* are you guys doing this?" I question through heaving breaths. My hands shake uncontrollably as my mind spins from trying to understand what is safe and what is to be feared. My hands shake uncontrollably and I shove at the door handle again, but of course, it doesn't budge.

Tears prick my eyes. *Fuck!*

Rook is beside me, one arm braced across the seat like a

barrier, not touching me, but close enough that I can feel heat radiating off him.

My eyes are wild as I look at him, and I reach out to shove him in the chest. But his chest might as well be made of fucking stone for as much good as it does. "Tell me what's going on!" I demand, voice cracking. "Right now!"

His gaze flicks to my face, then away again. Like looking at me hurts.

"Kylie," he says, low. "I'm sorry."

That makes my stomach turn colder.

"Sorry doesn't cover this," I whisper. "Those men…who were they?"

He doesn't answer.

"Rook." My voice breaks. "Who were they?"

His hand flexes once on his knee like he's trying to stay restrained, like he's trying to keep himself contained. "I can't explain it now."

"Pretty sure now is the perfect fucking time to explain it!" I scream. "There's no better time than right fucking now!"

"I'm sorry, Kylie. Not right now. We have to get somewhere safe first."

"Safe?" My laugh is maniacal. "Nothing about anything that's happening right now feels safe, Rook! Nothing feels safe!"

More tears prick my eyes when Rook doesn't respond.

Why won't he tell me what's going on?

Because he doesn't trust me? Because he thinks I'll scream? Because he's insane? Or because what he's about to say is worse than the part where three men tried to take me out of my own house?

I swallow hard. "Stop the car. Let me out."

His jaw clenches. "I can't."

"You can," I hiss. "Your brother is driving the car."

"I can't," he repeats, and I hear something final in it that makes my breath catch.

I stare at him, shaking, then glance toward the front seat where Kane's hands are steady on the wheel and Calloway's eyes are scanning the road like he expects company.

I don't know what I just got pulled out of. I don't know what those men in my driveway were trying to do to me. I only know I'm trapped in a car with three men I thought were just…guys.

And I don't know who I'm more afraid of.

14

ROOK

SHE DOESN'T STOP SHAKING.

Not when Kane takes the first turn too fast or when Calloway tells him we're clear. And not when the town disappears behind fog and trees.

Kylie sits pressed against the door, arms wrapped tightly around herself like she's trying to hold her body together by force. Her breaths come shallow and uneven, panic spilling through the cracks she doesn't know how to seal.

I keep my hands to myself even though everything inside me wants to reach out and pull her into my arms.

"Rook," she says, her voice breaking on my name. "I need you to tell me what's happening right now."

I don't answer. Not because I don't want to. But because telling her the truth means I'm shattering every sense of normalcy she's ever known.

Pretty sure you've already done that.

I steal a glance at Kylie, and tears shine in her big, beautiful eyes. Her breathing gets worse as she tries to hold herself together.

Her chest hitches like she can't get enough air, no matter how hard she tries.

"Hey," I say quietly. "Look at me."

She doesn't.

"Kylie."

"Tell me what is going on," she whispers, but her tone is sharp. "Tell me the truth, Rook! Tell me why three men were in my driveway this morning, trying to force me to go with them. And tell me why you stepped in and did God-knows-what to them and forced me to go with you." Her eyes are wild, and she bores her gaze into my skull. "Tell me!" she screams at the top of her lungs, and I don't miss Cal flinch from the high-pitched outburst.

"I know you deserve answers," I say, a sad sigh escaping my lungs. "But it's very fucking complicated, okay? And the short answer is that we're saving you."

"Saving *me*? From what exactly? Those men? Why wouldn't you just call the freaking cops?"

"Saving you from Holland Thorne," Cal chimes in quietly, his knee cocked and bouncing in the front passenger seat. "And those three men who are definitely connected to him."

"Saving me from Holland?" she snorts, her whole demeanor perking up with the ridiculous notion that this is all a simple misunderstanding. "How in the hell is Holland connected to those men? No! What are you guys talking about? It's fine! I know Holland. He's actually *nice* to me." She rolls her eyes at me and then proceeds to punch me a good fifteen times in the chest with both of her tiny, furious fists. "As opposed to the way *you* spend your time glaring across the rink and looking down your nose at me when you drive past my house. Or the fact that you just forced me into your car! You kidnapped me!"

I laugh. I can't help it. This whole fucked-up situation is so absurd it's becoming comical.

"I'm sorry to be the bearer of bad news, but you have no clue what you're talking about." I grind my jaw, and my voice shakes as I pound a fist into my own chest, the anger returning in full force. "Trust me, I'd rather not have to do this shit at all. I'd rather have some kind of say in *my* life too, but the nuts and bolts of it is that I don't. And you don't either. So here we are."

"What do you purport to know about *my* life that I don't?" she yells back. "Huh? You think you're some fucking psychic, Rook? That I don't have control of my own destiny? You don't know *fuck all* about me, much less what you *have to* do by *kidnapping* me, for Pete's sake! I gave you the benefit of the doubt before, but I'm done now. I will not be on tonight's news!"

She rolls down her window frantically, leaning out into the wind and screaming at the top of her lungs. We're the only car on this back road and there isn't a house in sight, but she keeps screaming in the hopes that someone will hear her.

"Kylie, calm down," I try to reassure, but she just screams harder and yanks on the door handle like she's fully prepared to dive out of a moving vehicle.

Though, Kane was smart enough to put the child locks on. He is also sly enough to roll her window up and lock it when she pauses her screaming to catch her breath.

But Kylie's hands are trembling now, fingers digging into her sleeves and her eyes darting to the windows like she's mapping escape routes that don't exist.

I lean closer, keeping my voice low, steady. "Kylie, breathe."

"Fuck you, Rook!" she screams directly in my face. "Fuck you!"

And then she starts sobbing into her hands.

When I try to touch her shoulder, try to calm her down, she pushes me away.

"I hate you!" she cries, and it breaks my goddamn heart. "Why are you doing this to me?"

Fuck.

She's spiraling. And I'm the reason.

15

Kylie

I NEED TO GET OUT OF THIS CAR.

I have no idea where Rook and his brothers are taking me, but I know they always teach women to never let them get you to a second location.

My eyes dart to the window again, the one I can no longer roll down because Kane put on the fucking child locks, and my brain struggles to form a coherent, logical thought that could get me out of this situation.

But there's no exit. There's no escape. And the only thing my body wants to do is scream.

So that's exactly what I do—loud and at the top of my lungs, and I don't stop.

I just scream. And scream. And fucking scream.

My ears can barely register Rook trying to calm me down, telling me to breathe and relax and whatever the hell else he's saying. I'm pretty sure Kane and Calloway are doing the same, but I just keep screaming.

"Let me go! Let me out of here!" I shout. "Let me fucking out of here!"

"Kylie, calm down." Rook's hand covers my mouth, and I twist and thrash against it, tears starting to fall of their own accord.

Please, God. I can't die like this. It can't end this way.

I fight as he pulls me into his lap. I fight as he pulls me toward him. I fight through one breath and the next and then another until, out of left fucking field and in the shock of a lifetime, his lips crash into mine.

He kisses me.

And suddenly, I *can't* fight anymore.

A shaky, broken sound slides out of my lungs like I've been holding my breath for hours. And my hands clutch at his jacket, fingers curling into the fabric like they need something solid to hold on to.

All the while, the panic drains out of my body in a rush that leaves my body melting into his.

Eyes closed and filled with tears, I marvel as an out-of-body experience consumes me and transports me through fire and light and stars and more. I feel like the world is spinning around me while I form my own, new axis.

I'm whole and warm, and all the fight inside me is extinguished completely.

I don't just feel compliant—I feel found. Whole. Like every single moment in my life has been a flash of orchestration, meant only to lead me here.

As Rook pulls away, his startled eyes and shaking hands giving way to a very real, raw fear, I start to tremble.

Reality is a figment—a lie. *Everything* is.

I don't even know my ass from my elbow, much less the meaning of my life or anyone else's.

I want to be the woman who's resisting—but she's gone.

I just wish to hell and fucking heaven and back again, I knew *why*.

16

ROOK

I DIDN'T PLAN IT. I DIDN'T THINK ABOUT IT. I didn't ask.

I just kissed her.

It wasn't soft or gentle or the way a man kisses a woman he's trying to charm. *No.* I kissed her with all the desperation I have for her, like I was physically trying to anchor her to me before she drifts away completely.

Now, her eyes are wide and her lips are parted and she's looking at me like she's trying to make sense of it all.

And every cell inside my body calls to her, wants me to kiss her again. Every instinct ingrained into my otherworldly DNA demands to be with her in the most intimate ways. And my mouth waters with the anticipation of knowing what she'd taste like if I sank my teeth into her neck.

Fuck.

"Rook?" Her voice is a whisper, and she mindlessly reaches up to touch an index finger to her lips.

"I'm sorry," I say, the words ripping out of me. "I shouldn't have done that."

She swallows hard. "Why did that…help? Why…why did it feel like that? Why… W-what is happening, Rook?"

Because you're mine. Because your body knows before your mind does.

"I don't know," I lie.

She studies me like she's seeing me for the first time. Like she's *really* seeing me. And I can feel that something has shifted. The space between us is no longer neutral. It's charged. It's awake. It's alive. It's fucking *pulsing*.

"You can hate me," I say quietly. "I won't stop you."

She shakes her head once, slowly. "I don't hate you."

Her gaze drifts to the window again, the trees blurring past, the world rushing forward without her consent.

"Where are we going?" she asks.

"Somewhere safe."

"You keep saying that." She lets out a humorless laugh. "But I wish you'd define safe."

I don't answer, because safe is a temporary condition right now.

Because I didn't just cross a line—I erased it.

Because whatever comes next could hurt.

Because I love her. Deeply, madly, and all-consumingly in a way you can't describe.

Because they are going to come for her. For me. For us. *And I'll let them kill me before I let them have her.*

17

THE HOTEL ROOM DOOR CLICKS SHUT BEHIND US, and the silence rushes in. But it's not a peaceful silence. It's the kind that presses on your ears until you feel like screaming just to prove you're still alive.

I don't know where Calloway or Kane went, but my mind was too scattered and overwhelmed to pay attention to the name of the hotel or try to overhear Rook's conversations with his brothers before they left.

Rook doesn't budge from where he stands near the door. He doesn't make a move to sit down on the bed or the small chair by the window. He doesn't say anything, tell me anything. He just freaking stands there while my mind reels in a million different directions.

I start to pace the room, still wearing yesterday's clothes, and when I catch a glance of myself in the mirror near the closet of the room, the feelings of shock and confusion and fear are quickly replaced by anger.

"So, this is it?" I snap. "You basically kidnap me without telling me why you kidnapped me after doing whatever it is you did

to those men at my house—the ones who were apparently trying to freaking kidnap me too—and you brought me here? To a
hotel room in I don't even know where, and you still aren't going
to explain any-fucking-thing to me?"

His jaw tightens. "It's temporary."

"Everything you've done today is temporary, apparently," I
fire back. "You don't explain, you don't ask, you just decide for
me."

I turn on him fully now, the fear from earlier burning off into
something hotter and sharper.

"You don't get to do that to me," I say. "You don't get to scare
me out of my own house, throw me into a car, and then expect me
to just…what? Calm down and go along with all of this insanity
without demanding some answers?"

"I'm not asking you to calm down," he says quietly.

"Oh good. Because that would be rich."

He exhales slowly through his nose, like he's counting to keep
himself in check. "I didn't have another option, Kylie."

"That's not an answer," I shoot back. "That's what people say
when they don't want to admit they took someone's choice away."

Something flashes in his eyes then—pain, maybe, or guilt—
but he doesn't interrupt.

Or give me any goddamn answers.

That makes me angrier.

"You know what's really crazy? I actually trusted you, Rook,"
I continue, my voice cracking despite myself. "I trusted you, and
now…I'm wondering if that was a serious lapse in judgment on
my part."

"Kylie, you can trust me. I would never, fucking ever, do

anything to hurt you. I'd let them ki—" He stops mid-sentence and then swallows hard.

Still, he's not telling me what the hell is going on.

I laugh once, but it's sharp and brittle. "God, you're unbelievable."

I move past him toward the window, then spin back around when the pull in my chest flares again.

"Why does it feel like this?" I demand. "Why does being near you feel like I can't think straight?"

His shoulders tense.

"Don't," he says.

"Don't what?"

"Don't ask questions I can't answer without making this worse."

"Everything is already worse!" I shout. "You kissed me in the car like it was the only way to shut me up. But God, the things it made me feel…" I pause and let my head fall back as the rush of emotions and feelings and sensations my body remembers from that kiss consumes me. I have to force a deep breath of air into my lungs before I can look at him again. "And now you're just… standing there. Just standing there and not telling me anything."

His hands curl at his sides.

"That kiss," he says carefully, "was a mistake."

The words hit harder than I expect. A mistake? *How was that kiss a mistake when it felt like everything?*

He looks at me then, and something raw moves behind his eyes. "It was a mistake because it made me want something I'll probably never get to have. Something I want and need more than anything in the fucking world but probably don't even fucking deserve."

All of a sudden, the room feels smaller. Every nerve ending in my body, every inch of my focus, homes in on him and the electric tension that vibrates between us.

My pulse stutters and my mouth goes dry. "What do you want, Rook?" I whisper.

"You, Kylie." His voice drops. "I only want you."

Something in me snaps, and I close the distance between us in two steps and launch myself into his arms.

I kiss him.

And it's not gentle or sweet. It's all teeth and frustration and a desperate need to feel in control of *something*. It's a vibrating instinct to feel all the things his kiss made me feel in the back seat of the car. It's an overwhelming need to crawl inside his body and become one with him.

His body goes rigid under my hands, and for one terrible second, he doesn't respond.

But then, he does.

He kisses me back. His hands come up to my waist, and his grip tightens on my hips like he's barely holding himself together. There's a heat in him that feels almost electric, like his body is shaking under the strain of restraint.

It makes me want more. Makes me want *him* more.

I press closer, my heart racing and my breath shallow, and I chase whatever this pull is that won't leave me alone. Recklessly, I ignore all the red flags and things that should most definitely be freaking me out, and I chase whatever is causing this blooming, undeniable, overwhelming need for him.

His mouth moves against mine, hungry and controlled at the same time, like he's fighting himself with every breath.

In this moment, I want to give him everything—my mouth, my tongue, my body, my heart, fucking everything that is mine.

But then he breaks the kiss and steps back as if he's been burned.

"Stop," he says, voice rough. "We can't."

The rejection hits harder than a slap to the face.

I stare at him, my chest heaving up and down in erratic waves. "You don't get to decide that either."

"Yes, I do," he snaps, anger flaring now. "When it comes to you, my willpower is already hanging by a fucking thread, Kylie. You have no idea what you're asking for when it comes to a man like me. When it comes to what is pulsing between us."

The implication hangs between us, heavy and frightening and intoxicating all at once.

It's all too much.

My eyes burn with emotion, tears threatening to flow down my cheeks at any moment.

But the most shocking part is that all I want right now is to launch myself at him again and give him every part of myself.

Never in my life have I ever felt like this about anyone.

And that's beyond terrifying. It makes me feel like I'm the girl in the horror flick who runs up the stairs when the psycho with the mask arrives at the front door.

Immediately, I turn and head for the bathroom, yanking the door open and slamming it shut behind me. I twist the lock hard enough to make it rattle.

"Kylie," Rook calls out, and tears start streaming down my cheeks.

"Leave me alone," I call through the door. "I need a minute without you deciding things for me."

The shower is on before he can say anything else. I remove my clothes, quietly sobbing the entire time, and step beneath the steaming spray.

Hot water pelts my skin, and I brace my hands against the tile, shoulders shaking as everything I've been holding back finally spills over.

Fear. Anger. Confusion.

And underneath it all is something worse—want.

I want him. *I more than want him.* It's as if I can feel my want and need for him pulsing in my veins. It feels as if each pounding beat of my heart is for his ears and only his ears. It's as if my mind and body are at war. It's as if I'm fighting every sane instinct inside myself not to run out of this shower and beg him to make love to me.

It's as if…deep down, I'm willing to do anything to be his.

And that is the most petrifying realization I've ever had.

I slide down the wall until I'm sitting on the floor, water streaming over me, and press my palm to my mouth to muffle the sound while I cry.

I don't know what he is.

I don't know what this is.

I only know that nothing in my life has ever made me feel this unsteady and grounded at the same time.

And that scares me more than being taken ever did.

18

THE BATHROOM DOOR STAYS SHUT.

At first, I tell myself she just needs a few minutes. Then an hour passes. Then two.

Steam curls out from under the door, carrying the faint scent of soap from her second shower, but also the scent of something sharper. She's scared and confused, and I'm hating every fucking second of it. I hate that I can't comfort her. I hate that I'm probably handling this all wrong.

I could read her mind if I wanted to. I could let myself get inside her head and hear everything that's rolling around there. But I just…can't invade her privacy like that. No matter how badly I want to.

I don't move from where I'm sitting on the edge of the bed, hands braced on my knees like if I shift, the whole situation might fracture again.

I don't knock. I don't speak. I don't try to coax her out of the bathroom.

I give her space. I learned a long time ago that hovering

doesn't help. It just reminds people they're not alone when what they need is the illusion of it.

Eventually, I stand and step into the hallway, grabbing the tray of soup and bread and bottles of water I ordered earlier from room service. I could've ordered anything off the menu—burgers, pizza, steak—but I decided to go with something light. Something that doesn't ask a lot of her.

I set it down outside the bathroom door.

"I have a tray of food out here for you, Kylie. You don't have to talk to me," I say quietly. "But please, eat something."

I'm only met with the sounds of her soft breaths. They're no longer tight and stifling like before, and I only hope that means she's no longer crying. *I pray that means she's not crying anymore.*

Eventually, the door does open, but any hope I have is deflated when she shoves the tray away with her foot and shuts it again.

Outright refusal, that's what Kylie Moon is giving me right now. And while I wish that weren't the case, I can't blame her. I can't fucking blame her at all.

I've made a real mess of this entire situation.

I leave the tray there anyway. Just in case she changes her mind.

Thirty minutes or so later, Kane knocks at the door. Cal's with him. Both of them look like they've been running. Their jackets are half-zipped, eyes sharp, scanning the hallway out of habit.

"How is she?" Kane asks, keeping his voice low.

"In the bathroom," I say. "Still."

"Well, shit." Cal grimaces. "That's not great."

"She asked for space," I reply. "She gets it. Pretty sure she deserves at least that much from me after all this shit."

Kane studies me. "And you?"

I shrug. "I'm still pretending to breathe."

That earns me a snort.

"Have you told her everything?" Kane asks, and I shake my head.

"Not yet."

Cal purses his lips. "Not trying to play back-seat quarterback, but I'm pretty sure she deserves the truth."

"I know." I sigh. "Trust me, I know." But fuck me, it's not easy telling someone everything they thought they knew about this world is a lie. It's not easy telling the woman who's your destiny that you're something she probably fears.

"We probably shouldn't stay here much longer," Kane comments. "Things are calm. They already cleaned up the mess in her driveway, but they're looking for us. They know." I can read between the lines—*they know, and they want us dead.*

"And the mess?" I question, and he knows exactly what I'm asking.

"Six feet under."

Yeah. I'm not surprised we killed them. When I saw that fuck trying to take Kylie, I lost it. I had too much rage pulsing through my body to do anything but end him. I'm also not naïve to the fact that taking out three of their gofers has only made us more of a target.

"We'll head out in the morning." I nod and look back at the

bathroom door. "I just want to give her a little more time before we move."

They exchange a glance.

"You're sure you want to give her more time?" Kane asks. "She's not exactly…thrilled anyway."

I almost laugh. "She doesn't have to be thrilled," I say. "She just has to feel like she isn't being hunted every second."

"And you?" Cal asks.

"I can handle it."

They nod, accepting that answer for what it is. I mean, it's certainly not reassurance, but it's resolve.

"We'll be back," Kane says. "Text if anything changes."

They disappear toward the elevator, footsteps fading across the carpet of the hall, and I shut the door behind me.

The room settles again, and I lie back on the bed, staring at the ceiling and replaying everything I shouldn't have done and everything I still will.

I don't know how long I lie there before the bathroom door opens.

Soft footsteps pad across the carpet of the hotel room, and when they stop, I feel the bed dip.

I turn my head, and I find Kylie sitting on the edge of the bed, wrapped in a hotel towel. Her eyes are red and her face is blotchy. Her hair is still damp from the third shower she took, and the strands curl softly near her shoulders.

She removes the towel and tosses it onto the chair near the window without ceremony. And I honestly don't even know if she realizes she's only in her bra and panties. It's as if she doesn't have the energy to care.

But she shocks the hell out of me when she climbs onto the bed beside me and curls her small body up beside mine.

"Rook," she says quietly.

"Yeah, Kylie?"

She hesitates, then shifts closer, pressing her forehead against my chest. "Just…hold me."

That's all she says, but right now, it feels like everything.

I slide an arm around her carefully, like she might shatter if I grip too tight. She fits against me instinctively, her breath evening out as soon as she's there, like her body's been waiting for this permission longer than she realizes.

I don't move.

I don't speak.

I just hold her.

Her fingers curl into my shirt, and her legs tuck against mine. The tension drains out of her shoulders and chest in slow increments. And eventually, her shuddering breaths give way to something that is deeper and softer.

She's asleep within minutes.

And I just lie there. Holding her and relishing the feeling of having her in my arms. Watching the door. Listening to the hallway. Counting the seconds until I have to tear us out of this fragile bubble and put her back into a world that wants to break her.

Tomorrow, we're going to leave here.

But first, she needs to know the truth.

And I make a promise to myself and to her that I'm going to give her all the answers I've been avoiding. She deserves that from me. She *needs* that from me.

After I tell her the truth, she might want nothing to do with me, but for now, she's warm and breathing and in my arms.

And that's enough to keep me still.

Because even though I already knew my reality, now I'm certain of it. I'd rather die than live in a world where she isn't mine.

19

KYLIE

I WAKE SLOWLY, LIKE I'M SWIMMING TO THE SURface of a warm pool of water.

The first thing I register isn't the unfamiliar room, but the solid, steady weight around me. Rook's strong arm is locked around my waist, firm enough that there's no doubt it's intentional, but gentle in the way it holds me there.

And all I feel is safe.

I don't move right away. I take stock instead. The stillness of his chest against my cheek. The heat of his body against my skin. The way his hand is splayed across my stomach, thumb resting just below my ribs like he put it there without thinking and never reconsidered.

I try to remember how I got here, in this room inside an unnamed hotel located at an unknown destination. My mind floods with memories of the three men in my driveway and the panic I felt when they tried to force me to go with them.

I swallow.

I still don't know what happened to them.

I still don't know why Rook and his brothers took me.

And I still don't know why my world felt like it tilted on its axis and exploded into full Technicolor flames when he kissed me in the back seat of the Suburban. Or why it felt even stronger when I kissed him in this hotel room yesterday.

I don't know anything except that I have never felt safer than I do right now, wrapped up in him like nothing could reach me without going through him first.

He shifts slightly, and I instantly know he's not sleeping.

I tilt my head back just enough to look at him, and his eyes are already on me—dark, alert, searching my face like he's braced for me to bolt.

For a second, neither of us speaks.

Something tight and electric hums between us, and a current runs under my skin. I feel tethered to him in a way I don't have language for, but it feels like if I moved away from him right now, if I got too far from him, something essential would snap.

I don't want to move.

I don't want to be anywhere else.

I shift carefully, turning in his arms until I'm facing him. His hand slides from my stomach to my back. He doesn't pull me closer, but he doesn't let go either.

I search his face for answers. For anything that makes sense of the way my chest aches when I look at him. The way my body seems to soften and brace at the same time, like it knows something I don't.

"Rook," I whisper.

"Yeah?"

I hesitate.

The kiss in the car flashes through my mind again—how

everything inside me had lit up, how the fear had burned away into something else entirely. But fear can do strange things to a body. Panic can blur lines and remove the capability of rational thought entirely.

I need to know why kissing him felt more necessary than oxygen. I need to know why kissing him felt like…my world just changed forever. I need to know why, even though I should be freaking out over this entire situation and the fact that I've just disappeared from my life and how Martin is probably losing his mind that I haven't shown up for work, but all I can think about is *him* and how my body wants to crawl inside his skin.

So, I kiss him again.

It's careful and testing at first. My lips brush his, waiting for my body to tell me if this is real—or if it was just adrenaline and terror masquerading as something deeper.

However, the moment our mouths meet, that same fire roars back to life, but it's even hotter and steadier than before. It floods me, head to toe, like every nerve just came online at once.

I kiss him again and again, each time more certain, more desperate to understand what's happening to me.

His arms tighten around me, muscles coiling under my hands like he's holding himself in check with sheer willpower. He kisses me back with a restraint that feels almost painful, like he's standing at the edge of something and refusing to step over it.

When I finally pull away, I'm breathless and trembling.

"Why…why does it feel like this? Why…" My voice shakes uncontrollably, overrun with every hidden feeling I've ever suppressed toward Rook and the big, *different* life I dreamed I'd have, and then some. "Why, Rook? Why?"

His forehead drops to mine.

"You're mine," he says quietly. "And I'm yours."

"Says who?" I challenge, even as warmth blooms deep in my chest at the words.

He lets out a breath that sounds like surrender.

"The universe," he says. He shakes his head, like he still can't quite believe it himself. "You and I, Kylie Moon, we're meant to be. We're destiny."

My heart stutters.

"We're fated mates."

20

ROOK

SHE DOESN'T STAY IN MY ARMS LONG. NOT BEcause she pulls away in fear, but because she needs space to process and think and try to wrap her mind around things that contradict the foundation and reality that her entire life has been built on.

Of course, I let her have it. She deserves to fucking have it.

I watch her slide out from under the sheets, wrap herself in the hotel robe, and cross the room with careful steps, like the floor might shift under her if she moves too fast.

She sits on the chair with her hands folded in her lap, eyes wide and glassy, not crying but not steady either. Just…processing.

I stay where I am, on the edge of the bed, giving her room without putting distance between us. Every instinct in me wants to close that gap, to pull her back and remind her she's safe—but I don't.

She needs this moment to be hers.

She's not so much upset anymore as she is overwhelmed, and for that, I can't blame her. The whirlwind she's been dragged into would challenge anyone, but to be put in this position without any prior knowledge is akin to something like taking a bar exam without having ever cracked a law textbook.

But I know where *I* stand.

Whatever this thing is between us—whatever lit up the second she came into my life—I've stopped pretending it's temporary. She's mine. I'm hers. I don't question that anymore.

What I question is what I've set in motion by choosing her first and taking her before they could.

The danger I've now put us in. Put my brothers in. Put her in.

"I'm supposed to be at my grandmother's tonight," she says quietly. "Dinner. Staying over. But I don't even have my phone to call her. I don't know if she's tried to call me. I..." She pauses, and worry creases her brow.

"I know."

Her head snaps up. "You do?"

"Yes," I admit. "And she's going to hear from you. Your phone—everything you left behind—we'll get it for you. Nothing about this ends with her worrying where you are."

"Okay." She nods and stares down at her hands in her lap again.

And I let the silence linger for a little bit, giving her more time to wrap her mind around it all.

"I know this is a lot," I eventually say. "It's been...a lot for me too. And I know I haven't handled it well or set you up to feel comfortable now in any way, but I... Well, I'm willing to answer anything you want to ask, unfiltered, of course, and now that you're safe, I'm also willing to give you space. Not a lot of space," I hedge. "Like...the next room, but it's better than—"

"I don't want space," she says suddenly, her eyes snapping to mine and cutting me right to the quick. There's so much fire there—so much feeling. If it weren't an exact mirror of my own emotions, I'd probably struggle to understand the depth of it.

But the kisses between us…they broke something. Or, I don't know, built it, I guess, depending on how you look at it.

Our bond, as it were, is fully formed.

She's still confused and hurting—but she trusts me. Her body demands it.

"Okay. Then I'll be close. Ask me whatever you want, and I promise I'll do my best to answer it. I'm afraid if I try to explain it all myself, I'll just overwhelm you."

"I…well, I don't really know what to ask, so I guess I'll start the only place I can."

I nod encouragingly.

"Where…where are we right now?" she asks. "I mean, I know we're in a hotel room," she says through a self-deprecating snort as she glances down at the robe she's wearing. "But what hotel?"

"The Westin. Worcester, Massachusetts." My smile is soft, and her eyes widen at the sight of it. I know it must be a shock after months of angry looks and monosyllabic grunts, but it's amazing how much more peaceful I feel now that I've given in to the universe's pull.

"Right. And…why are we here?"

"Because it's safe right now. Distant enough Holland and the others won't be able to sense us."

She giggles, and for far from the first time, I try to insert myself into her level of naïveté. It's hard, to say the least, but I was there once. As a young boy, I had no idea why I craved the smell of blood or moved so much faster than those around me. As a young boy, I often thought of myself as a freak show.

"Hah. Right. *Sense* us. So, when you say that, you mean…"

"Smell, visions. Just overall intuition. We're—our kind—is gifted in all sorts of ways."

"Right, right." She sucks her bottom lip into her mouth for a long moment before quietly asking, "And by *your kind,* you mean…?"

The word is a whisper and a bomb all at once. "Vampires."

Her giggle turns chaotic as she jumps from the chair and starts to pace, turning back to me for confirmation every so often. I hold myself still and steady, waiting for her to be ready for more before continuing.

When she sits back down, she does it right next to me, pushing the heat of her thigh into the heat of my own for comfort.

My throat thickens instantly with want, but I shove it down.

"Vampires," she whispers, testing the word on her tongue.

I nod. "Vampires."

"Like…vampires in the way I'm imagining them? With bloodsucking tendencies and bats and glittery skin…"

"Minus the bats," I say. "And closer to Dracula than anything sparkly. But the basics are relatively the same."

"So, you need…*blood*…to survive?"

"Some vampires do, but they're becoming an extinct breed."

"What does that mean?"

"There are vampires who have been turned from humans, and there are vampires who are born into this world. I was born into this world, as are most of the vampires you've come into contact with in your daily life. It's seen as a highly taboo practice for a vampire to turn a human now."

A shocked laugh bubbles up from her lungs. "Well, I'll be honest, I didn't even know vampires existed until exactly one minute ago, so…yeah."

"We blend in," I tell her. "On purpose."

"So…you and your brothers were born…like humans are born?"

"Yes."

Her jaw drops. "That's…*how*?"

"Vampires can mate with humans, Kylie. But they have to be the right humans with the right bloodline."

"Can you…turn me into a vampire?"

"Sure." I shrug. "If I wanted to."

"But you don't want to do that?"

"Fuck no." I shake my head. "I'd rather off myself than do that."

For a moment, her mouth turns down at the corners, and I furrow my brow as I take in her reaction.

"Are you disappointed?"

"I…" She blows out a breath. "Don't know what I am right now."

"The idea of changing anything about you is abhorrent to me," I tell her and mean every single fucking word. I just want her. In all of her perfect humanness.

She nods and digs her teeth into her bottom lip. "So… vampires like you don't need blood to survive?"

"No. And we don't need human food either. Think of us as kind of self-contained battery packs, I guess."

"Well, if you don't need blood to survive, what do you need it for?"

I shrug. "Power. Pleasure. Longevity. And in some cases, healing. It's an enhancer. And blood like yours…is the best."

"So, I have good blood?"

I nod, and my mouth waters at the mere thought of her perfect, tempting blood. "Good isn't a strong enough word for your blood, Kylie."

"Human blood can heal?"

I nod.

"But I thought vampires couldn't die…?"

"Once we turn twenty-eight, we age at a much slower rate than humans, but we can die. Not easily and only at the hands of another vamp, but we can."

"How slow are you talking about?"

"We can live centuries. There are vampires out there who are five hundred years old."

She pauses for a long moment. "And you said *pleasure*?" she asks, and her cheeks flush red. "In regard to…uh…drinking human blood."

I smile. I can't help it. Everything about the word rolling off her tongue is exciting. "Yes. Sucking blood from your mate during intercourse can be *very* pleasurable. For both the human and the vampire."

She studies me for a beat, then stands and crosses the

room. She walks slowly, like she's deciding something with every step.

When she stops in front of me, I don't move.

She lifts her hands and cups my face, searching my eyes like she's looking for something final. Something concrete. "I think…I think I need to experience it to really understand."

I lean down, lips brushing her ear. "Are you asking me to make love to you, Kylie?"

She nods. She's not sheepish, not even unsure, but her breath hitches in her lungs.

"You have no idea how badly I want to," I murmur. "I want to put myself inside you and never fucking leave."

She shivers.

"But once I do," I say, my voice growing rougher, "there's no going back. Not ever."

Her brows knit together. "What do you mean?"

"It means the first time won't just be sex." I trace her delicate jaw with my thumb. "And, well, I can smell that you're still untouched. Still a virgin." I lean down to brush my lips against her ear again, whispering, "Our first union binds, Kylie. It seals us. Permanently."

She blushes. "You *know* I'm a virgin?"

"That and about a thousand other things, Ky." I search her eyes and watch as her mind calculates everything I just told her. "We're fated mates," I add quietly, but there's no lack of power or conviction in my voice. "Our first union would be as binding as an inked and sealed contract. It would bond us forever. It'll make you mine, and me yours, until the end of the mortal world and won't be broken even a second before. And because of the power of the bond, the aging process will slow inside you too. You'll live much longer than an average human."

"And if we don't?" she asks earnestly.

"We'd feel this anyway." I reach out to run my fingers through the silky locks of her pretty hair. "Every day. Every second. The pull would just get stronger. And we'd just be fighting against it until the day we die."

"I already feel *bound* to you," she whispers. "Like I'll die if you leave this room."

Fuck. Me too.

"Option number one sounds like a whole lot more fun," she adds softly.

A dark laugh rumbles out of me. "Yeah," I agree. "Fucking tell me about it."

"Rook…" She holds my gaze with her own and puts a palm to my cheek until the whole room around us feels like it melts away. "I need you. I want you. Take me."

"Say it again," I demand because, fuck, I feel like I've been waiting ten lifetimes for this.

"Make love to me, Rook."

At her words, I know I've never felt anything lock into place like this.

Never felt anything that has ever compared.

I don't step away. I don't pause. I *react.* I give in to my throbbing need for her.

I walk her backward until the backs of her knees hit the mattress, and she falls back into the sheets with a gasp escaping her lungs. Her brown hair fans across the pillow, and her gaze holds mine with laser focus.

I follow her down, bracing my weight so I don't crush her, even though every instinct inside me wants to take and claim and devour.

And the entire time, her blue eyes are locked on mine.

"Still time to run," I murmur.

She lifts her chin, shaking her head as she reaches out her hands to grasp my shoulders. "Not happening."

That's all I need.

My mouth finds hers, but no matter how gentle I'm trying to be, I know it's not gentle at all. It's not patient or tentative. It's intense, it's deep, it's claiming.

She makes needy sounds that feed my desires even more, and I move my lips to her neck, smelling the heady scent of the blood racing through her veins and pressing my lips against the frantic rhythm there. Her heartbeat stutters against my tongue when I lick at the pulsing skin.

Fuck me. Her blood. It's my fucking drug. It's my own personal siren's call, and every cell inside my body wants to sink my teeth into the delicate skin of her neck.

But I don't. I *won't.* Not unless she wants me to. Her safety, her comfort, her well-being trump any desires I have.

She's not just mine to claim. She's mine to keep. To protect.

Mine, mine, mine. All mine.

In this moment, there's no internal noise over Holland Thorne or the gofers and their plans, or the elites and their claim over Kylie and the other two of *the three bloodlines.* All of that is outside, with Kane and Cal as they trail and recon.

There's no world outside this room.

Only this. Only *her.*

And I can see the beauty in it now—this twisted, powerful thing I've been fighting since turning twenty-eight—and the significance in the perfection of it all.

To be fated—destined—is a feeling like no other in this universe. A *gift*.

Not a curse like I previously thought at all.

"You're so beautiful," I tell her, meaning it in ways language can't contain. "There will never be a more beautiful thing to me. Nothing in this world will ever compare to you."

Her lips part, and my mouth moves to the thrum in her neck again. But this time, I just rest it there, memorizing the beat and the rhythm of the life that flows inside her.

And begging the universe to keep it that way until the world is no more.

I draw a path of kisses from her neck to her chin, and I don't stop until I fuse our lips together again. Light and aura dance through the darkness behind my eyes, and waves of indescribable warmth roll through my chest.

I drag my mouth from her throat to her chin and back to her lips, and when I kiss her this time, it isn't exploratory. It's raw and primal. She pulls at my shirt like she's trying to climb inside my skin, and when her fingers can't move fast enough, frustration flashes across her face.

With swift motions, I tear through the fabric of her robe and her panties.

She gasps, but it's not in protest. It's in hunger.

"Rook," she breathes, and the desperate, downright needy way she says my name makes something feral break open inside me.

I strip myself bare without breaking eye contact. The entire time, her gaze rakes over my body—my shoulders, my arms, my stomach, *my cock.*

And then, she opens her legs. For *me.*

Her gaze deliberately locked with mine the whole time.

Kylie's bare, pink, perfect pussy is right there, spread wide for my eyes—for my cock—and I can smell her arousal. I can hear the throb of her sensitive flesh.

Every inch of her body is pulling to me like gravity.

I move over her, framing her face in my hands and pressing my forehead against hers for a half second that feels eternal. The tip of my cock just barely brushes against her already wet entrance, and I swear I would forget to fucking breathe if my lungs actually needed oxygen.

Instead, a deep, guttural growl jumps from my throat.

"Show me I'm yours," she whispers.

And I can't deny her. Will probably never be able to deny her anything she wants for the rest of forever.

She pulls my face down to hers and kisses me with an intensity that makes my cock jolt toward her body. She moves her hips against me, and I don't have an ounce of restraint left in my body to hold back.

I push inside her.

I fill her tight pussy with my rock-hard cock.

And the world doesn't explode—it fucking *locks.* Every cell, every nerve, every piece of matter inside my body attaches itself to everything that is her—memorizing her scent, her breath, her heartbeat, her eyes, her lips, her body, her fucking everything.

She looks up at me, eyes wide, lips parted, and I see it.
She feels it too.
The seal. The bond. The permanence.
Kylie Moon is mine now.
Forever.

21

ROOK'S THROAT FLEXES WITH HIS ROAR AS HE thrusts himself inside me. The sound that leaves him is not human. It's not loud or performative, but low and rough and feels as if it's pulled from somewhere primal. Somewhere ancient.

I moan and grip the flesh of his shoulders with my fingernails. They indent and bend the skin, cutting through to the next layer, but no blood comes out.

It's a reality check of what he is—and, surprisingly, a rush like I've never experienced. There's something about bringing something greater than man to his knees and reaping the spoils. And with the way he explained it, this moment means that power is mine to wield forever.

This man isn't fragile. He's not breakable. He's a beast, and it feels like he could crush every bone in my body with his fucking pinkie finger.

That only makes me wetter, and I feel the ease with which his cock slides in and out of me. The sounds of my arousal mix with the guttural sounds of his thrusts.

And his cock. Holy hell. It's big. It's hard. And it's throbbing inside me. *I want this man to fuck me like this for the rest of my life. As long as he keeps doing this, I will do anything for him.* Anything.

His mouth is set in a firm line, and the cut of his jaw showcases a restraint that must weigh a thousand pounds. He's holding back. He's not giving me everything, but goodness, I want *everything.*

The way my pussy tightens around him, the way my hips shake and my muscles tremble, the way my body reacts to him, isn't something I have control over. It's instinctual, as if my body and his body were meant to do this. As if we were made for each other.

"Rook," I whisper, my body tight and rubbery all at once. Stars dance behind my eyes as he begins to move, and every primal piece of me I didn't know existed begs for him to sink his teeth into me.

His eyes darken. The brown of his irises deepens—shadows cutting through them like something intense inside him is stepping to the surface.

"You feel it," he says.

"Yes."

This is my first time making love to anyone, let alone Rook—and yet, it feels more natural than anything I've ever done in my life. It feels like breathing oxygen but also needing the oxygen to stay alive.

It makes it easy to believe him when he says we're each other's destiny—every part of me can feel it.

And I just want to keep doing this. I want to stay connected to him like this forever.

But then Rook is sliding out of me, disconnecting us completely, and a half moan, half whine bubbles up from my lungs.

He kneels between my spread thighs, his hard, throbbing cock in his hand and my arousal dripping off it. And he stares at me, his eyes raking over every inch of my face and my breasts and my hips and my body.

But when his eyes fixate on the heat between my legs, his tongue sneaks out, licking across his bottom lip.

"Rook, please," I beg. "I need more." *I need everything.*

He lifts his eyes, meeting mine with an intensity that makes my breath catch and my hips tilt toward him. "What did you just say?"

"I need more."

He shakes his head. "What did you just *think*?"

I hesitate, but then I whisper, "I need everything."

His cock jolts forward at my words, like his body is literally trying to climb back inside me. And I just watch the erotic scene that is him stroking himself and staring at me while panting breaths vibrate my chest.

Can you hear my thoughts? I think.

He nods.

You can hear everything I'm thinking right now?

He nods again.

You can read minds?

"No, not like this." He shakes his head. "This is different. It's the bond. It's…because you're mine." He lifts my hips up so they're resting on his thighs, and he rubs the tip of his cock in circles against my clit.

Fuck, I have to hold back. This kind of intoxicating want is dangerous. I fear I'll destroy her if I let go. The thoughts slip into my head, but I know they're not mine. They're *his.*

I want her mouth and her tits and her pussy and her perfect fucking ass. I want to fill her up with my come. I want to sink my teeth into her neck and feed off her. I want to claim every inch of her body until no one can touch her without knowing she's mine.

I lock our gazes, my eyes searching his. "Don't hold back," I whisper. "Claim me. Take everything. Take it all."

Rook stills, and I can hear his mind working overtime to understand what is happening. *You can hear me?*

I nod.

Our bond is so strong, Kylie. And fuck, I'm starting to fear how much I want you.

Don't, I respond. *Just let go.*

He slides the length of his cock between the lips of my sex, not inside me but still pressing against my highly aroused flesh in ways that make more moans escape from my lips.

And I'm mesmerized by the sight. My eyes fixate on the hardness of his cock and the strength that lies in his forearm as he grips himself.

"What do you need, Kylie?"

When I don't answer, he reaches down, gently puts his fingers under my chin, and lifts my eyes to his. "What do you need?"

I look at him. But I don't say it out loud. *I need your cock inside me, stretching me, filling me. I need you to fill me up with your come. I need fucking everything. I. Need. You.*

A growl escapes his lips, and he lifts me to sitting with a gentleness and an ease I don't think I'll ever get used to. My legs are sprawled out over his thighs, and his cock is perched right at my entrance.

We're face-to-face now, his dark and heated gaze locked with mine.

"Fuck, I don't think I'll ever have enough of you," he says, his voice deep and throaty in a way that makes my nipples harden. He leans down and sucks one of my breasts into his mouth while he jolts his hips upward, driving deep inside me in one steady thrust.

And it's this biting combination of pleasure and pain. Euphoria and purgatory. But the pain isn't from this being my first time; it's from the realization that I don't know if I can ever get enough of him. It doesn't matter that he's well-endowed and his cock is stretching me to my limits—I don't think it'll ever be deep enough.

Simply put, I will never get enough of him. I will spend the rest of forever wanting more. Always wanting more.

There's a masochistic part of me that wants you to tear me apart. That wants you to take every single thing I can give you. I would bleed myself dry for you.

"Stop," he growls, lifting his head to meet my eyes.

But when he tries to stop the movement of his cock, I take things into my own hands and start riding him myself. And the more I ride him, the wetter I get, the arousal turning so obscene that I can *hear* it as I move myself up and down.

"Kylie." He groans. "Fuck."

"Don't hold back," I whisper. "Please, please, please don't hold back."

"You don't know what that means." His jaw tightens. "You don't know what you're asking for."

"Then show me."

"*Kylie.*"

I reach up to grab his face between my palms, forcing his gaze to mine. "Don't. Hold. Back."

His cock throbs inside me. His grip on my hips grows tighter. And every time my panting breaths make my breasts brush against his chest, I feel his body tense up.

"Don't hold back," I repeat. "Claim me, Rook. Taste me. Feed on me."

"*Kylie.*"

"Feed. On. Me."

On a growl, his restraint fractures. He lowers his mouth to my throat, and when I feel the press of his teeth, I don't tense. I relax. I open up. I fucking bloom.

The bite is sharp, and then heat pours through me like molten lava.

It doesn't hurt. It *ignites.* My breath shatters into something desperate and needy, and my body reacts to the feeding as much as to the way he's moving inside me.

The connection amplifies. Every sensation doubles, and I feel it in my arms and my legs and deep, deep in my core where the connection of the two of us burns.

His groan vibrates against my skin, deeper now, and edged with hunger.

You have no idea what you do to me, Kylie, he thinks.

I just want to be yours, my mind whispers to him. *Forever.*

And he sucks gently at my neck, feeding off my blood, while he continues to thrust his cock inside me.

My eyes fall closed, and my senses fall over a cliff of rapture.

It's not like the orgasms I've given myself with a vibrator or my hand—it's beyond any earthly thing I've ever experienced.

It is cosmic and celestial and transcendent of this universe and the next.

Rook Slater and I aren't one person—but we should be.

His groan is low and deep as his tongue lashes over the wound at my neck and forces it closed, and despite the continued pleasure of our connection, I miss it.

I can see how I could get addicted to it—how he could have me begging for it day in and day out. Because I already want him to do it again. And again. And again. Self-preservation is no longer a thing. I'm reckless in my need for him.

"You're mine," he says against the new and tender flesh, and I nod vigorously in reply.

"I'm yours," I agree.

His mouth finds mine and takes me in a kiss so intense, I almost lose track of everything else. Of the room, of the world, of time and space and matter.

"You're mine," I whisper when he's done, testing out the words on my tongue and loving them instantly.

They aren't just nice—they're perfect.

"I'm yours," he agrees. "In this world and the next and everything in between, Kylie Moon. I'll be yours until time no longer exists."

I wake to the smell of pot roast.

And the realization hits before I open my eyes, sinking deep into my chest like a weight I didn't know I'd been carrying. The air is warm and familiar, laced with rosemary and onions and something sweet I can't quite place.

I sit up too fast, heart slamming against my chest while the quilt covering my body slips down my waist. And instantly, my vision is filled with the sights and memories of the place I called home for most of my life.

Gammy's house.

My eyes dart around my old childhood bedroom, taking inventory of pink walls and floral curtains and the old oak dresser with the chipped corner I used to stub my toe on as a kid.

"How…?" I whisper, and when I look toward the window, I find Rook sitting in the chair I used to curl up in when I was a teenage girl sneak-reading my grandmother's Harlequin romance novels.

He has a notepad and pen in his hand as he scribbles furiously at an inhuman speed. When he notices my open eyes, he freezes completely.

"How…how did we get here?" I ask. Last thing I knew, I'd fallen asleep in the hotel bed, my legs intertwined with his much larger ones after making love for the first time.

His smirk is smooth and cocky as he raises a shoulder. "There are a lot of things I'm capable of that are going to come as a shock to you at first. Some of them you learned yesterday. Some of them you learned this morning."

"And what?" I snort. "You couldn't, say, do the kidnapping this way, with your super sleuth-y voodoo vampire magic? Slide in while I was asleep on the couch, have us avoid the whole violent battle with three ominous men in my driveway, and wake me up with a coffee or something?"

He chuckles, and butterflies dance in my chest at the sound. It's *beautiful* and so intrinsically satisfying. To be honest, I don't think I'll ever get used to it.

"A fair point, and a far better plan than I executed myself," he admits with a smile. "But you have to understand, before you were mine, I knew you were *supposed* to be. Fighting against it robbed me of every ounce of my finesse."

"And why *did* you fight it?" I ask then, my voice soft. "If we're so meant to be, why didn't you just…flirt? Let it happen?"

Standing slowly, he sets his pad and pen to the side and walks to the bed to lean over me with his hands at my waist. His eyes are calm, but his lips are tight as he touches them to mine. "Get dressed," he says cryptically instead of answering. "Some of this… is better heard from someone else."

"Someone else? Someone else who?"

The question is barely out of my mouth before he's out of the room, flashed down the hall in a blurred cloud of speed.

Annoyed and intrigued at once, I climb out of the bed, throw on the blue and yellow striped matching sweats he's laid out at the foot of it, and make quick work of peeing and brushing my teeth before heading down the hall.

When I get to the kitchen, my grandmother and Rook are both sitting at the kitchen table, waiting for me. Even knowing we're at her house, and that it makes sense for her to be here, the sight of the two of them sitting there so casually comes as a complete shock.

But the second Gammy sees me, she's on her feet.

"Oh, baby."

She crosses the room in two steps and pulls me into her arms, holding me so tight my breath catches. Her shoulders tremble, and when she presses her face into my hair, I feel the dampness of tears.

"I was so scared," she whispers. "I tried to call you yesterday and this morning. You never answered. And I thought—"

"I'm here," I murmur, clinging back just as hard. "I'm okay."

She pulls back, cupping my face with both hands like she needs to see me whole to believe it.

Only then does her gaze slide to Rook. Something complicated crosses her expression—relief first, then fear, then something like resignation.

"So, Rook," she says softly. "You think it's time we tell her?"

"Yes, ma'am," Rook replies.

"Wait…you know Rook?" I ask, looking between them, still trying to catch up.

"Not until a few hours ago, sweetheart, no. But I've known of him—and of *his kind*—for quite some time."

"Vampires," I say on a whisper, and it's so tragically comical, even Rook has to hide his smile.

My grandmother, though, she laughs outright.

"Yes, dear. Vampires." She eyes me knowingly. "Now do you see why I've been trying to get you here so hard so we could have a talk?"

"*This* is what you wanted to talk to me about?"

"Well, I wasn't pulling your leg, sweetheart." Gammy sighs and nods. "But hopefully, you can see now why I thought it best that we have this discussion in person."

I snort. "I probably would have had you committed."

"Mmhmm," she hums before jerking her thumb at the coffeepot behind her. "Make yourself a cup and sit down. We still have quite a bit to talk about."

I move to do as I'm told, but Rook is faster—obviously—jumping up from the table, pouring a cup, and mixing in cream and sugar for me before I can even make it to the counter.

He holds it out to me slowly, and I get up on my toes to touch my mouth to his, grateful that he had the foresight to bring me here. I'm biologically comfortable with him now—*clearly*—but hearing the kinds of things I can only imagine I'm about to is still so much better from a familiar face.

Escorting me to my seat, he pulls out the chair and waits for me to get comfortable before taking the one next to it this time.

I don't miss Gammy's subtle smile or the satisfied way she hides her face behind her own coffee mug when Rook asks, "You good?"

I nod. "As good as I'll ever be when my grandmother's getting ready to tell me alien ships are waiting in the ocean to take us to another planet, and when we get there, we'll be the king and queen of the society."

Rook smiles, and I shrug. "Am I close at least?"

"No." He shakes his head softly. "But I'm thoroughly entertained, and that isn't easy, so good job."

"Thanks," I say smugly, sucking in a sip of the most divine coffee I've ever tasted. Rook isn't only as fast as the speed of light, strong as a superhero, and so capable of producing orgasms I'm still walking funny—he's a regular barista too.

"All right, sugar, time to get down to the hard stuff. As you know now, we humans are far from the only thing in this big world.

It makes sense that we'd think so—what with how self-centered we tend to be—but we're not. Not even close. Rook, his brothers—"

"Holland and the rest of the Fighting Fangs," Rook jumps in to supply.

Gammy nods. "They're all vampires."

I nod self-consciously, still feeling wild for believing it all. "Rook told me."

"Well, what they didn't tell you about, I'm told, is another group of vampires you haven't met—the elites."

I grimace. "Let me guess. Untouchable money. Untouchable power."

"Untouchable because no one ever sees them. They don't show up in headlines. They don't need names." Gammy's jaw tightens. "This group of vampires doesn't believe they're obligated to follow rules or a code or any of the worldly order of any of the others, and as such, they take what they want without asking."

"What do they take?"

"Humans," Rook growls. "Women. Like you."

My eyes grow wide as they jump to Gammy, who's nodding along slowly. She reaches out and grabs my free hand, and I put down my mug to sandwich her fingers with the other. "Women like me?"

"Our family is part of a royal group of humans, honeypie. A very powerful heritage known to Rook's kind as *the blood of the three.*"

"Okay, yeah, I don't like the sound of that *at all.*"

"Of course you don't, baby. You're a woman born of rebellious blood. Your mama—she was the same way."

"What do you mean? Mom…Mom was part of this?" My voice shakes, and my lip quivers slightly.

"Think biologically, Ky," Rook suggests softly, cupping my shoulder with his strong hand. "If you're of royal blood, so was your mother."

"But your daddy wasn't, sugar," Gammy explains. "He was human. A regular guy with a regular job and a sweet, sweet smile. And because she was in love, your mama thought she could buck the rules—go her own way. And they killed her for it."

"So…you're saying the same people—vampires—responsible for killing Mom…want me?" Gammy's frown is all the answer I need. My whole body shakes as I admit, "Gammy, you're scaring me."

"Time to be scared is long past, baby doll. This is the time to be brave. To fight. It's the only chance you have. Because as soon as Rook took you as his mate—as soon as he followed the universe's plan instead of theirs—baby, he set off a war like you've never seen."

"A war. Over me."

"And well, well beyond. This isn't a disagreement, honey. This is a clear line in the sand that these men—honorable men like Rook and his brothers—aren't going to let the elites have their way anymore. And that's why you need to stick by Rook's side now. He'll protect you. He'll keep you safe."

My stomach drops. "This is almost too much to wrap my mind around." I look between Gammy and Rook. "What does this mean for my life?" I shake my head back and forth. "My job? *Oh my God.* Martin is probably freaking out that I wasn't at work yesterday. And he has a wife and kids and…and…and…" The more my mind races, the more my voice rises in discomfort. "And Alyssa. I don't want anything to happen to Alyssa."

"They're safe," Rook says. "I promise you, Kylie. They're safe."

"But you have to cut ties with them for now," Gammy chimes in, and my chest grows tight with discomfort.

"Cut ties with them?" I question. "How the…I don't even know—"

"I'll handle it, dear," Gammy says like it's the simplest thing in the world to do.

"Gammy, you're acting like it's as easy as returning a horrible Christmas gift," I retort. "Alyssa is my best friend. And Martin, well, I honestly don't know how he's going to survive the rest of tax season if I just disappear. I wouldn't be surprised if he's already filed a missing persons report when I didn't show up yesterday."

"Dear, I've already spoken to Martin. He thinks you're ill." Gammy walks over to wrap me up in a tight hug. "I know this is a lot," she whispers into my ear. "But remember, Kylie, this isn't just for you. It's for them, too. This is how you keep everyone safe."

Tears prick my eyes. "And what about you?"

"Oh, honey," she says and squeezes me tighter. "I'll always be in your life. Maybe a little differently than we're used to for now, but I'll always be here."

I stay in Gammy's arms for a long moment, but eventually, my mind starts to catch up with the seriousness of this situation.

"What does this mean for you, Rook?" I ask, meeting his steady gaze. "That you intervened?"

And for a second, I see *him*. Not the vampire or the fighter, but the man who chose me.

"It means they won't let this go," he says. "It means I stepped in front of something powerful." A small sigh escapes his lungs. "It means they'll come."

A chill crawls up my spine. "Come for what?"

"For me."

His eyes lock with mine, and I see no fear or hesitation there. But goodness, the room feels smaller. Hell, I'm certain the walls are starting to close in on me.

"They want me dead, Kylie."

The word dead doesn't echo; it settles permanently into my bones. My heart starts to pound so hard and fast inside my chest, I can hear it in my ears.

But we just got each other yesterday, I think, panic slipping through the bond before I can stop it.

I know, baby, he answers inside my head, his voice steady and sure and calm in a way that's hard for me to understand. *And you are the best thing that's ever fucking happened to me. But taking you was the equivalent of signing my warrant,* he continues. *Holland, his cronies, the elites behind them—they all want me dead.*

His jaw tightens, but his gaze never wavers from mine. And his eyes show no ounce of fear.

But my entire body is quaking with fear.

Somewhere beyond the walls of Gammy's house, some of the most powerful men in the world are deciding how to kill him.

22

ROOK

THE CABIN SITS WHERE THE ROAD GIVES UP. It's located high in the mountains and far enough north that the air sharpens and the pine trees grow bigger and thicker.

This, right here, is deep New England wilderness, the kind people talk about but don't actually go looking for.

We built this cabin ourselves years ago. Me, Kane, and Calloway. We hauled the beams, laid the foundation, and cut the forest back just enough to be able to reach the cabin but still keep it hidden. At the time, I thought we were just building a place to get away, someplace to allow ourselves to go completely off-grid.

In hindsight, it's almost as if we were preparing for something we didn't know we were preparing for.

It's nearing midnight. Kylie and I came straight here after Gammy's. We didn't take any stops or detours, and a trip that would take hours by car took us a fraction of that by the speed of my feet. Vampires are fast. Some would say inhumanely fast. And I can vouch that's very much the case. Though, genuinely speaking, when the goal is to blend in, showcasing otherworldly speed and strength is something we keep under wraps.

Clearly, the cat's out of the bag now. At least with Kylie.

Cal and Kane are still working to get intel. And thanks to their help, I'm certain no one followed Kylie and me here.

Our cabin is truly in the middle of nowhere. There are no neighbors and no lights beyond the small lamp on the porch. There's not even much of a cell or Wi-Fi signal unless you know exactly where to position yourself to get it.

Kylie stands on the porch behind me, arms wrapped around herself, eyes studying everything. I watch on in fascination as her gaze takes in the wooden beams of the cabin, the stone chimney peeking out from the roof, and the faint glow from the windows inside.

I could read her mind right now, but I don't want to do that.

I want to give her space to make her own observations and let her decide if this is a place that could feel like home.

Though, when the silence stretches out into the forest, I can't stop myself from asking.

"What do you think?"

"I love it," she says, a soft smile covering her pretty mouth and her eyes meeting mine. "It's...cozy and rustic and...like something out of a fairy tale. I think I'll gladly stay here with you. For as long as we have to."

"I'll take care of you, Kylie," I tell her, and I mean every fucking word. Safety, money, food, human needs, I will do whatever it takes to provide and protect. "You have nothing to fear, okay?"

"Okay." Her nod is hesitant, and I lean forward to press my lips to hers.

"I love you."

"I love you too," she whispers and presses another small kiss to my lips. Then a giggle escapes her throat. "Though, in a strange way, the word love doesn't feel like enough."

I laugh. I can't help it. "I know exactly what you mean."

Her smile lights my whole world on fire, and I take her hand, guiding us inside the cabin.

Instantly, the smell of woodsmoke and pine surrounds us. Kane and Cal came by earlier while Kylie and I were at her grandmother's, so a fire is already going in the fireplace.

I glance around at the familiar surroundings—the thick rug on the hardwood floor, the worn but cozy couch in front of the fireplace, the kitchen table and chairs Kane and Cal made from pine trees.

Everything here was built to last. To shelter. To protect. There are even three bedrooms with attached bathrooms in the cabin— one here on the ground floor, one below in the basement, and one upstairs.

Honestly, looking back, it's almost comical how prepared we are for this very situation.

Kylie sets down the bag my brothers grabbed from her house—clothes, her phone, her laptop, toiletries—and turns slowly, taking it all in. "Where are Kane and Calloway?"

"Doing what they need to do," I say. "Watching. Listening. Making sure no one gets close to us."

Her mouth curves in a small smile that doesn't quite reach her eyes. And her shoulders dip like the weight of everything has room to settle now that we're alone.

"Kylie," I say quietly.

She turns—and then she's moving.

She crosses the room in three quick steps and throws herself into my arms. Her arms lock around my neck like she's afraid I'll disappear if she doesn't hold on tight enough. She presses her face into my chest, and I feel the heat of her tears soak through my shirt.

I can't lose you, her mind whispers.

And I don't hesitate.

I wrap her up completely, one hand cradling the back of her head, the other firm at her waist, while I hold her shaking body steady against me.

"I know you said I have nothing to fear, but I'm scared, Rook," she whispers through shuddering breaths. "Everything you and Gammy said…it's all so big. And dangerous. And I…" She sucks in a breath. "I just can't lose you. I can't fucking lose you."

I pull back just enough to look at her.

Her eyes are red and glassy and full of fear she's been holding back since we left her grandmother's house this evening.

"You're not going to lose me," I say firmly.

She shakes her head. "You don't know that."

"I do," I reply. "Because us not being together isn't an option. My entire being revolves around you and me, Kylie. I'll do everything I have to do to keep you safe."

Her hands clutch at my shirt like she's anchoring herself. "Rook—"

I cut her off with a kiss.

And I kiss her like I mean it when I say she's safe. Like I mean it when I say I'm not going anywhere. She kisses me back with the same intensity, her fear bleeding out into the space between us until all that's left is heat and need and the quiet understanding that we've chosen each other.

When I lift my head, I rest my forehead against hers.

"I'll carry the fear," I tell her. "All of it. You don't need to."

Her lips tremble. "You can't do that alone."

"I'm not alone," I say. "I have you."

That seems to settle something in her.

She kisses me again, and when I lift her into my arms, she lets out a small laugh through her tears and wraps her legs around my waist as if it's the most natural thing in the world.

I carry her to my bedroom—*our* bedroom—down the hall, kissing her the entire way.

I lay her on the bed and slowly remove our clothes.

Nothing about this moment is rushed. It's slow. It's steady. And it's focused on us. On just being together.

When I slide my hard cock inside her, she's wet and aching and needy, but I don't move with haste. I move with care and gentleness and every ounce of love I feel for her.

"Feed on me, Rook," she whispers into my ear before pressing her neck to my lips.

Her blood calls to me like a fucking beacon. And my mouth is already watering at the thought of sinking my teeth into her skin and tasting her. Hell, it only makes my already hard cock harder.

But I swallow down the urge and lean my forehead against hers, locking our eyes while I continue to move my cock inside her.

"No," I say gently. "Not yet."

She frowns. "Why?"

"Because I'll never take from you at the expense of your well-being," I tell her. "Not tonight."

She studies my face, and I hear her mind trying to find a way to get me to feed on her. She wants it as much as I want it; I have no doubt about that. But her safety and health will always come first for me. I simply can't feed on her if I feel it'll make her weak.

"I love you," I tell her. "Fuck, I more than love you, Kylie."

"I more than love you too, Rook."

Eventually, we come together—slowly, deliberately—letting the world outside the cabin walls fall away. The fire crackles. The night presses close. And for the first time since this all began, I let myself believe that here, in this place, she's truly safe.

I hold her until sleep takes her again. And I spend the rest of the night listening to the quiet thrum of her heartbeat and the steady breaths of her lungs.

All the while, my mind makes a firm decision—*I will fucking burn down anything that dares to take her from me.*

23

I WAKE UP SMILING.

The fire in the hearth has burned down to embers, painting the cabin in low orange light. Rook's arm is still wrapped around me like a steel bar, heavy and sure, as if it hasn't moved once since I fell asleep.

The clock on the nightstand reads **3:14 a.m.**

I wiggle just enough to test a theory, and he doesn't stir. Not even a little. And I tilt my head back and find him already looking at me.

"Were you just…watching me sleep?" I ask on a whisper.

"Yes." He smiles, and there's no embarrassment or hesitation.

"Oh boy." I giggle. "That's either incredibly romantic or incredibly creepy."

"Depends how you feel about it."

"Definitely romantic. Though, maybe it should be a red flag?" I roll onto my side, propping myself up on my elbow so I can see him better. "Pretty sure most serial killer documentaries start with someone creepily watching another human being sleep."

His chest shifts with a surprised laugh, and that leads to

several hearty chuckles escaping his lips. Grumpy, surly, always-super-serious Rook Slater laughing? Man, I love that sound. Want to spend the rest of forever hearing that sound.

"I can assure you, I'm not a serial killer," he says with an amused smile. "But I won't deny I love watching you sleep. I also love watching you smile." He reaches out to run his index finger across my currently smiling mouth. "And laugh. And talk. And do pretty much anything at any given moment of the day."

"So…you're obsessed with me?" I ask, my smile turning teasing.

"Oh baby, I'm more than obsessed with you."

I don't miss the fact that he looks exactly the same as he did hours ago—alert, calm, eyes dark and focused like the night hasn't touched him at all.

"You're not tired tonight," I note.

"No." He smiles again. "Vampires don't get tired."

"What do you mean by that exactly?"

"I mean, we don't need to sleep."

I search his eyes. "Like at all?"

He shakes his head.

"So…every time I'm sleeping…you're just awake? Holding me for hours?"

"Yes." He presses a soft kiss to my forehead. "And there's no other place I'd rather be."

Warmth presses against my rib cage, and I touch my palm flat to his chest, feeling the solid heat and steady strength of him.

"You know, that feels wildly unfair," I murmur. "You don't need to eat, you're basically running on unlimited batteries, *and* you're, like, a supernatural weighted blanket."

His mouth twitches. "Not everything in life is fair, baby."

"No, not everything in life is fair," I say. "But at least we have each other."

"Forever," he agrees, and the urge to kiss him, to touch him, to be as close to him as I physically can, overcomes me.

I kiss him. My mouth light and teasing and my teeth playfully nipping at his bottom lip.

And when a soft groan escapes his mouth, I climb over his body and straddle him. His hands move to my hips automatically, gripping the flesh gently. His cock is already hard; I can feel the bulge of it against my panties.

I roll my hips, using his arousal to press against the bundle of nerves between my legs until a little moan escapes my lips.

"Careful," he warns, and I just playfully roll my eyes at him on a snort.

"You're the one who said forever, Rook. You can't threaten me now."

"Damn, Ky." He laughs again. "You're dangerous when you're sassy."

"You should remember that," I say, leaning down to press my lips to his. "I'm a very dangerous girl, and it would be in your best interest to do what I want so you don't get hurt."

I roll my hips against him again, slow and deliberate, and he grips my hips tighter, forcing me to stop.

"*Kylie,*" he chastises, all serious Rook again.

"You know what? You're grumpy when you're turned on."

A smile twitches his lips. "And you're a handful."

"A handful that's tired of your mind-blowing restraint."

He just laughs. "Restraint is important, baby."

"But I don't want you to exercise restraint right now." I lean down, my mouth brushing his ear. "I want you to lose control. I want you to feed on me. You wouldn't do it last night."

"No."

"Why not?" I ask, leaning back to meet his eyes.

"Because I'm not draining you for sport."

"But that's what I want, Rook. I want you to feed on me again."

He shakes his head. "I don't want to weaken you, Kylie."

"But it doesn't make me weak," I whisper and brush my mouth against his. "It makes me feel things I can't even describe. Good things. Amazing things. Things that make me wet whenever I think about them." I reach down and slide my panties out of the way of my sex and roll my hips against him. Letting him feel my heat. Letting him feel my arousal. "See? I'm already wet right now."

"Fuck, Kylie." A groan escapes his lungs, and he briefly shuts his eyes.

"I want to feel you inside me. I want to feel you feeding on me. I want all of it, Rook. I need it. Badly."

His gaze locks with mine. Hunger, fear, protectiveness, they all flash across his face at once.

"Rook, stop holding back," I whisper, and my hips just keep humping erratically against him, my entire body greedy for him. "Stop holding back and put your cock inside me. Stop holding back and feed on me."

For half a second, I think he's going to refuse. But then, he flips us in one smooth motion, pinning me beneath him without crushing my weight, his body warm and solid and very, very aroused.

"You're bossy."

"You love it."

"I do." His mouth hovers near mine. "But you're playing a dangerous game, baby."

Heart racing and completely unafraid, I let a moan escape my lips. "Do your worst."

"The good girl and the bad man," he whispers.

"You're not a bad man, Rook."

"Kylie," he says quietly as he brushes his lips against mine, "you underestimate what I'm capable of when it comes to you." He leans back to meet my eyes, and he drags his thumb slowly across my lower lip. "I don't hurt people without reason." He slides his hand to my neck, fingers resting over my pulse. "But you're not a reason." His voice drops. "You're the line."

"And if someone crosses the line?"

"I'd kill them."

His teeth graze across the skin of my neck, and my pulse jumps in anticipation.

"Do it," I whisper and wrap my legs around his waist, forcing his cock inside me by shifting my hips. I'm already so wet that he slides in easily.

And then he sinks his teeth into my neck. The bite isn't painful, though. It's fire. It's ecstasy. It's heat rushing through my veins and exploding in my chest.

He starts to thrust inside me, each drive of his hips backed by power and hunger and strength. He pushes himself as deep as he can go, stretching me to my limits, and his mouth sucks at my neck, taking drop after drop of my blood.

I feel so much pleasure I can't contain my moans or panting breaths.

No restraint, Rook feeds on me. Fucks me. And feeds some more.

And all I feel is heat. Our bond. And the unwavering certainty that there is no world in which we untangle from each other now.

I can't live in a world without him.

24

ROOK

KYLIE SITS BAREFOOT ON A KITCHEN CHAIR. Her hair rests on her shoulders in adorable, messy waves, and she's wearing one of my shirts like it belongs to her.

She takes a bite of eggs and hums, eyes closing in appreciation. "Okay," she says. "This is unfair. You shouldn't be able to cook this good when you don't even eat the freaking food."

I smile and walk over to put a freshly cooked piece of bacon on her plate. "And just think, you haven't even tried the bacon."

She takes a bite, and a little moan escapes her lips. "Totally unfair, Rook."

Sunlight slips through the cabin windows in pale gold bands, catching on the edge of the table and the cast-iron pan on the stove. Mornings out here in our wilderness cabin are quiet in a way that only makes you feel peace.

Before Kylie, I would often come here by myself just to feel something. Before her, before our bond, I didn't feel much of anything besides annoyance. Irritation. And a lot of times, total apathy.

But she's changed all of it. Turned my world on its fucking head. She makes me feel like I'm finally *living.*

"Baby, I think you're looking at it the wrong way." I toss a wink at her over my shoulder. "I mean, you have your own personal vampire chef now."

"Yeah, okay." I look over my shoulder to find her grinning around a mouthful of eggs. "Maybe it's not so unfair."

I laugh, and I can't stop myself from walking back over to her and leaning down to press a kiss to her lips. She tastes like coffee and salt and morning, and the feeling that rolls through me is so intense it may as well be a living, breathing entity.

I'd burn the world for her without hesitation.

There's no undoing what we've done. When fated mates consummate, it locks. It binds. It's permanent. The elites can't breed her now. They can't even use her blood for pleasure or power or strength.

If they'd try to drink from her, they'd risk their own death.

The past few days, Kane and Cal have been rotating watch and moving in the shadows. They stayed local to listen and track and try to gauge retaliation.

To the elites, I took something that didn't belong to me. And worse—I made sure it can never belong to them.

Last update Cal gave me was yesterday evening. He said he's definitely heard shit—threats, posturing—but there are no actual plan in place yet.

But to me, that doesn't mean safety. The elites won't just forget about this. Not a fucking chance. Right now, they're calculating. They're figuring out their next move.

Bottom line, they want me dead. And they probably want Cal and Kane dead too.

To them, Kylie isn't an asset anymore. So if they still tried to get her, it would be to kill her. Just like they did with her own mother. And that realization is a dark, dark thought. It's so dark that I make a concerted effort not to let it sit in my head. Because of our bond, Kylie can read my thoughts just like I can hers.

And the last thing I want to do is scare her.

"Hey…" She reaches up, fingers curling into my shirt, tugging me closer. "Where'd you go?"

I shake my head. "Nowhere for you to be concerned about."

She quirks an eyebrow. "You're hiding something from me."

I don't lie, but I don't confirm either.

"Rook," she says, her gaze searching mine the entire time. "You're actively keeping me out of your mind."

"Yeah, I am," I admit. "But it's because there's some shit I don't want to fill your head with."

She examines my face for a long moment, and I can actually feel her trying to get inside my thoughts.

Don't keep stuff from me, Rook, her mind whispers inside my own. *Whatever is happening, we're in this together.*

I know, baby. I know. But just trust me on this, okay? Right now, I don't want you thinking about this shit.

Is this about the elites? The ones who want to kill you.

I nod.

Promise to tell me eventually?

I hesitate, but when she narrows her eyes, I nod. Anyone else, and I wouldn't have any issues lying to them. Keeping shit from them. I would tell myself it's for their own good, and that would be that.

But with Kylie? It goes against everything to lie to her.

"More than love you, baby," I tell her, and a soft smile crests her lips.

"More than love you too." She rises to her feet and gets on her tippy-toes to press a soft kiss to my jaw.

But I can't stop myself from taking it further.

Without hesitation, I lift her into my arms—her legs wrapped around my waist—and I kiss her. I back her toward the counter, resting her ass on the top of it, and my hands settle at her hips as I deepen our kiss.

The pulse between us explodes, and that kiss turns into a frantic mess of lips and tongue and teeth and hands.

"Rook," she breathes.

I rest my forehead against hers. "Tell me to stop."

She doesn't.

She slides her hands into my hair, and her mouth finds mine again. I deepen the kiss, every instinct urging me forward, the world narrowing down to this—her warmth, her trust, the certainty pounding through me.

And I'm about to have my wicked way with her right here on the kitchen counter when the sounds of footsteps echo inside my ears.

My head snaps up, every sense flaring.

Kylie stiffens. "What—"

"Stay here," I murmur, already turning toward the door.

But when it opens, Calloway steps inside like he owns the

place—which, to be fair, he does. His gaze flicks from the table to Kylie on the counter to me standing far too close.

"Thought I'd check in to see how it's going." A slow smile spreads across his face. "Clearly, it's going well."

I roll my eyes. "You have horrible timing."

Kylie snorts.

And Cal pulls out a chair and sits at the table. "Still nothing major on the radar. Our names are being dragged through the mud. A lot of death threats, but no organized movement yet. I'm confident we're safe here for now."

I nod. "Where's Kane?"

Cal shrugs. "Should be here shortly. There's one more thing he said he needed to check on."

The morning moves forward after that. Kylie finishes her breakfast. Cal gives me more updates about what Holland and the other gofers are currently plotting and scheming.

And for the most part, everything feels good.

Until a few hours later, that is.

The door slams open, and Kane bursts in with a woman slung over his shoulder.

Holy fuck.

She's thrashing in his grip, her arms flailing and legs kicking. Her mouth is wide open in a scream that never makes it past her lips, eyes wild with terror and fury.

"What the fuck?" I snap.

Cal is already on his feet. "Holy shit, Kane!"

"She's fine," Kane says, breathless but controlled. "I mean, she's real fucking pissed at me, but she's fine. She's safe."

Kylie's eyes are wide as she looks between Kane and me and

the unknown woman on Kane's shoulder. I don't hesitate to stand up and move across the room to wrap my arm around Kylie's shoulders. Her body shakes with concern.

"Who is she?" Cal asks, and Kane has to adjust his grip as the woman fights harder against him.

"Her name is Blair."

Blair's eyes meet mine—panic bleeding into disbelief—and something hits me like static.

Her thoughts. I can hear them. They're disjointed and fragmented and fear tangled up with expectation. She's thinking about elites and vampires and shouting that she's going to kill Kane. And her mind is filled with names that belong to very fucking powerful people.

I freeze. "Kane, why do you have her?"

"I had to," he says. "I had to save her."

Blair tries to scream again, but still, nothing comes out of her mouth. And when I look at Kane again, I'm certain her silenced screams have something to do with him. He's controlling them. How, I don't know, but he is.

"She thought she was being chosen," Kane adds. "Thought it was an honor. A fucking privilege. She was just going to walk into the viper's fucking den willingly. She has no idea what they were planning to do to her."

"Fuck me." Cal sighs. "You met her at the preview, didn't you?"

"What preview?" I question, but both of them ignore me.

Kane just stays silent and Cal looks enraged.

"I can't believe you fucking kept this from me, Kane," Cal

snaps, but Kane doesn't back down as Blair continues to thrash her body on his shoulder.

"She didn't know the truth, Cal! She thinks it's some kind of fucking fairy tale! Her goddamn mother was helping her shop for fucking clothes!" Kane shouts, his eyes wild with unnamed things. "I couldn't not step in. I couldn't not save her. I had to. I fucking had to."

But the more he speaks, the more I see the look in his eyes, the more I start to realize.

"Fuck, Kane," I mutter. "Fucking fuck."

"She thinks she knows," he continues. "But she has no fucking clue. I couldn't let her go there. I had to stop it."

"You're locked in," I whisper, and Cal's face whips to mine. "This isn't just any woman, Cal. This is *her*." *His fated mate.*

"Oh fuck." Cal's eyes go wide, and he looks back at Kane. "Oh fuck, fuck, fuck, Kane. Do not tell me this is what I think it is. Please, do not fucking tell me."

"Cal, you remember when you asked Rook if it was immediate with Kylie?" Kane questions, but it's clearly rhetorical by the certainty in his green eyes. His mouth curves into something between awe and dread. "Well, I can confirm that it is, in fact, immediate."

Silence crashes down around us, and the air instantly feels heavier.

This isn't just about me anymore.

This isn't just about Kylie.

As Blair bucks silently over Kane's shoulder and Cal's hearing stretches outward, straining for threats that haven't arrived yet, I understand with brutal clarity.

Something major has shifted. And the pattern is accelerating.

The change occurs when male vampires turn twenty-eight. Only then are their bodies ready to find their fated mates.

But Kane isn't twenty-eight yet.

However, he just kidnapped a woman who has very clear ties to some of the most powerful men in the world because he didn't have any other option.

Because of the bond.

Holy fuck. The shitstorm I thought I'd created by taking Kylie has just strengthened tenfold.

This isn't the end; it's just the beginning…

Read *Repo Man* today!

(The next book in the Blue-Collar Vigilante Vampire Series)

You know you want to read Kane Slater's book…
Read Repo Man today!
This is the next book in the highly addictive Blue-Collar
Vigilante Vampire Series!

Check out the entire series here:
Blue-Collar Vigilante Vampires
https://geni.us/BCVV_Series

Sign up for our newsletter, and we'll keep you up-to-date on
any **exciting vigilante vampire** news, AND a lot of times, we
share fun teasers and excerpts for our upcoming releases!
www.authormaxmonroe.com/newsletter

Need EVEN MORE Max Monroe?
Check out our Suggested Reading Order on our website!
www.authormaxmonroe.com/max-monroe-suggested-reading-order

Follow us online here:
Facebook: www.facebook.com/authormaxmonroe
Reader Group: www.facebook.com/
groups/1561640154166388
Twitter: www.twitter.com/authormaxmonroe
Instagram: www.instagram.com/authormaxmonroe
TikTok:_vm.tiktok.com/ZMe1jv5kQ/
Goodreads: https://goo.gl/8VUIz2

Acknowledgments

To all the most important people in our lives.
You know who you are.
We couldn't do this without you.
We love you.

To all our reader friends, THANK YOU FOR READING. You're the best.

And last, but certainly not least, to our dream team. The people who surround us and help us turn our words into books. The people who help us reach our readers. The people who support us every step of the way in this industry. Mark Gottlieb, Lisa Hollett, Stacey Blake, Kim Greene, Rick Hambright, Peter Alderweireld, Joanne Cote-Felaccio, Kristina Hassaker, and so many more amazing people, we are forever grateful for you.

XOXO,
Max & Monroe